"...Joyride is by no means joyless ... scores in its delineation of relationships, as old, and as complex as time."
Jeffery Gantz
The Boston Phoenix

One of the hottest young playwrights in the province.
Andy Pedersen, The Daily News
May, 1995

Melski scores big with Hockey Mom, Hockey Dad ... you'll hear them laughing a lot ... Masterly ... It is funny but potentially tragic as well ...
Everything about this play works ...
Stephen Pedersen, The Chronicle Herald
February, 1995

Enthralling ... Caribou is brilliantly written ... [Melski] shows so much promise that he is the playwright in residence at the Shaw Festival this year.
Peter Fenwick, The Eastern Star
July, 1995

...Fringe Offers Joyride You Won't Want to Miss ... a rare find ... searing, funny, unflinching ... Brilliantly crafts humor into a dark despair ... Gutsy, uncompromising theatre ... a must.
Elissa Barnard, The Chronicle Herald
September, 1994

Tender, understated ... [The Trout Fisher's Companion] is a treat for its moving truthful look at male bonds, Maritime life, and the power of love and imagination to answer need.
Elissa Barnard, The Chronicle Herald
April, 1993

Blood on Steel

Michael Melski

University College of Cape Breton Press
Sydney, Nova Scotia 1996

University College of Cape Breton Press
Box 5300
Sydney, Nova Scotia
CANADA B1P 6L2

Cover design by Goose Lane Editions, Fredericton, New Brunswick.
Book design by Gail Jones.
Cover photograph by Ron Blanchard.
Back cover photograph of author by Bruce Adams.

Printed and bound by City Printers, Sydney, Nova Scotia, Canada

---

Canadian Cataloguing in Publication Data

Melski, Michael, 1969 -

Blood on steel

Contents: Joyride - Heartspent and black silence.
ISBN 0-920336-80-9

I. Title. II. Title: Joyride. III. Title. Heartspent and black silence.

PS8576. E58B56 1996   C812'.54   C96-950046-7
PR9199.3.M45B56 1996

DEDICATION

This book is dedicated to my grandparents:
Mike and Christine Dezagiacomo, and
the late Anne and Andrew Melski.

ACKNOWLEDGEMENTS

I am grateful to many people, without whose support and/or wise counsel, this publication would not have come to pass. Many thanks to Dr. Rod Nicholls and Penny Marshall at the University College of Cape Breton, Liz Boardmore, Weldon Bona and the Dangerous Dreamers Company, Linda Moore and Neptune Theatre, Mary Vingoe and Eastern Front Company, Paul Dervis and Karen Marek at Theatre Redux, Anne Marie Melski and Scott Banks, Cailey Stollery, Steven Manuel, Irene Poole, Shannon Sponagle, Allister Jarvis, Frank Flynn, Jean Morpurgo, Scott Christensen and Michelle Horacek.

The actors who I have been fortunate enough to work with have all contributed a great deal to my understanding of the scripts. Their advice and talent have been golden, and their commitment to the work has been an inspiration for me to drive on. Thanks.

These texts are slightly revised from their original productions. These revisions were begun during the latter part of my residency at Shaw in July-August 1995. Much appreciation to the Shaw Festival Academy, including Christopher Newton, Neil Munro, Gie Roberts, and Denis Johnson.

For their generous support of my work in the past year, I graciously acknowledge the contributions of the Canada Council, the Ontario Arts Council, and the Nova Scotia Film Development Corporation.

Most of all, I thank my mother and father, Mary and Bernie Melski, for the well of love and support they have always provided. Without them, I would not have been born, and certainly would not have survived this long, as a writer or otherwise.

"Searching, blinded.
For two days I groped over them and called them.
Then hunger killed where grief had only wounded.
When he had said all this, his eyes rolled.
And his teeth, like a dog's teeth clasping around a bone,
Bit into the skull and again took hold."

-Seumas Heaney
from Ugolino

Table of Contents

Author's Notes

Joyride began, appropriately enough, in a car. In late spring of 1994, I returned home from Toronto, and caught up with my best friend, Paul Beaton. We spent an evening shooting the Sydney drag in his souped-up burgundy camaro, drinking Tim Horton's coffee, and looking around for someone on the streets that we knew. We were too old for this familiar ritual, but we didn't have anything else to do.

And we didn't seem to find anyone. Most of our old friends had moved off the island looking for work. Nothing new in that, but the young faces that were hanging out that night seemed strange to me. There was something a little scared, a little desperate that kept occurring in the eyes. It was two years after the McDonald's murders. But the wake wasn't over. Maybe it never will be.

Heartspent and Black Silence started during a period when I was looking for work in Toronto, and happened to scan a Greenwood racing form. I remembered winning big at Tartan Downs one night years before when I was in my teens. Then I remembered losing big for several nights in a row afterwards. As Nova Scotia's first casinos were being built in September 1994, Mary Vingoe, a self-admitted shit disturber, encouraged me to write this script.

Cape Bretoners have always been gamblers; the first of our ancestors who arrived here to stay gambled they'd make it through the winter alive. Five hundred years later, things haven't changed much. The Island's obsession with games of chance remains a reliable subject for farce and satire. In fact, it is frequently tragic. Gambling is a parasite, feeding on the last straws of faith. Carried to extremes, it is a glamorous deception; a "midnight express" to the darker places in the heart where nothing is sacred or tame.

M.M.

JOYRIDE

Characters

JESS in his early 20's

RACHEL in her early 20's

CRAIG in his early 20's

Setting
Various locations around Sydney,
Nova Scotia, over a few days in mid-spring.

Joyride was first produced by Caution to the Wind Company at Cafe Ole, as part of the 1994 Atlantic Fringe Festival in Halifax, Nova Scotia on August 31, 1994.

JESS   John Beale

RACHEL   Michelle Horacek

CRAIG Martin Burt

The production was directed by Shannon Sponagle.

SCENE 1

Hardwood Hill Cemetery. Evening.

[RACHEL, seated on a stone marker.]

JESS: (*entering*) Hey.
RACHEL: Hey.
JESS: Craig not here yet, is he?
RACHEL: He's late. He said he was comin at 6:30.
JESS: Was he supposedta come early?
RACHEL: I'm not early for him.
JESS: No?
RACHEL: No.
JESS: Ya know Craiggie. He's always late for everythin.

[pause]

RACHEL: Just so ya know, Jess, I'm not waitin for him.
JESS: I never said ya were.
RACHEL: I never said ya said I was. I'm just tellin ya.
JESS: I didn't say nothin.
RACHEL: I never said I wanted ya to. So shut up about it.
JESS: I never said nothin about you an Craig.
RACHEL: Ya don't have ta say nothin when I know what
    you're thinkin.
JESS: Rach. Ya don't know what I'm thinkin about.
RACHEL: I do so. Just don't suffocate me, okay?

JESS: I won't.
RACHEL: Fine.

[*pause*]

JESS: So what are ya doin now?
RACHEL: What does it look like I'm doin. I'm sittin. I'm
　　　doin squat.
JESS: Why'd ya wanna meet up here in the graveyard
　　　anyways?
RACHEL: I don't know. It's central.
JESS: I guess so.
RACHEL: We usedta play up here, remember?
JESS: The cops chased us out all the time.
RACHEL: I know. An we weren't even doin anythin illegal.
　　　Just hangin.
JESS: *(sitting)* Ya can see the wholea town from up here.
RACHEL: Yep. Ya sure can.

[*pause*]

JESS: This'd be a good place ta go. If you were goin out
　　　with someone.
RACHEL: Sure. Ya got a great viewa the steel plant an the
　　　slag heaps. It's real romantic.
JESS: It's peaceful, though.
RACHEL: Peaceful. It's fuckin paralyzed, is what it is.
JESS: Whaddya got there, rum an coke?
RACHEL: [*passes it*] I hate cops. They kick ya outta the
　　　cemetery for disturbin the peace.
JESS: Thanks for savin me some.
RACHEL: ...An it's only a buncha dead people around who
　　　can't hear ya anyways.

[*HE spits it up.*]

JESS: This ain't rum an coke, Rach.

RACHEL: I know. I took a bottlea pop from the store an I grabbed the wrong bottle.

JESS: What is it?

RACHEL: Morgan an Root Beer. It's disgusting.

JESS: Why didn't ya just take it back? Ya work there.

RACHEL: Jess. I took the bottlea pop. I stole it.

JESS: Oh. Ya stole it.

RACHEL: It's not like I can go, Dan, can I please exchange this, how bout a refund?

JESS: Do ya think Dan knows ya took it?

RACHEL: Na. He's dumb as a post. He's a bonehead.

JESS: Rach. Ya got caught doin that before.

RACHEL: Hey. Workin at that hellhole, I deserve a little treat now an then.

JESS: Yeah. I guess ya do.

[pause]

RACHEL: Don't gimme that tone. You're not so lily white yourself.

JESS: I never said I was.

RACHEL: Ya think you're McGruff the fuckin crime dog? I got lots on you.

JESS: Oh yeah? Not much, ya don't.

RACHEL: Remember when we were little we useta play the shopliftin game?

JESS: Well, I wasn't very good at that game.

RACHEL: Ya had ta steal bigger an bigger things every time. It was great.

JESS: I got caught with a boxa jumbo Tide detergent. I barely got away.

RACHEL: Ya shoulda just walked out with it. Ya can't conceal a boxa Tide.

JESS: Yeah. I shoulda went for the small box I guess.

RACHEL: Once Craiggie made it outside with Dan's hearin aid. I don't know how.

JESS: Really?

7

RACHEL: He didn't get far though. Craiggie was always in trouble.

[*pause*]

JESS: Do ya think youse two'll go out again?
RACHEL: I don't know. I ain't psychic.
JESS: I'm just askin.
RACHEL: Ya don't haveta worry about me. I can take carea myself.
JESS: Why's he comin back home now?
RACHEL: He said on the phone the judge gave him probation.
JESS: Oh.
RACHEL: But they're makin him live with his stepdad. Craig hates his guts.
JESS: I heard his stepdad is pretty tough.

[*A car screeches down below them.*]

RACHEL: Speakina arseholes, there goes Ronnie Coste an his new Patsy.
JESS: How'd ya know it was him?
RACHEL: I know the sound of a camaro.
JESS: Who's Patsy?
RACHEL: All his girlfriends are named Patsy.
JESS: Yeah?
RACHEL: Yeah, if ya let Ronnie smack ya around a bit, he'll let ya ride shotgun.
JESS: Y'know. Ya got a lousy taste in guys, Rach.
RACHEL: Oh yeah? Least I go out. Who'a you ever gone out with lately?

[*pause*]

JESS: I go out with you. I never met many new people lately.
RACHEL: Y'know why? Cause you're always hangin out with me.

JESS: So...I like goin out with you.

RACHEL: Jessie, you're waitin for your ship ta come in at the airport.

JESS: Oh, why don't ya just eat me?

RACHEL: Lookin for a meal not a snack.

JESS: Don't go chasin after guys just cause they drive Camaros.

RACHEL: Why shouldn't I?

JESS: Cause. There's a lotta real morons out there drivin camaros.

RACHEL: An lotsa good guys...

JESS: It's only a fuckin car, for Chrissake.

RACHEL: ...Drivin lawnmowers?

JESS: Ya dirty bitch.

RACHEL: Oh Jessie take me for a drive on your power mower!

JESS: *(laughing)* Dirty bitch. DIRTY DIRTY DIRTY Bitch...

RACHEL: I know I am...Never said I wasn't.

JESS: *(yelling)* RACHEL CLARE GIVES THE BEST HEAD IN CAPE BRETTTON..!

RACHEL: ...YOU'RE FUCKIN-A RIGHT I DO.

JESS: ...TA DOOOONKK-EYYYS!

[*SHE wrestles him.*]

RACHEL: I'll fuckin kill ya and bury ya up here.

JESS: RAPE RAPE RAPE RAPE..!

RACHEL: Yeah. Don't you wish.

JESS: Hey, don't stop I was just gettin into it.

RACHEL: We're not kids anymore.

JESS: Yeah. I know.

[*SHE sits.*]

RACHEL: Y' know somethin? I'm gonna be buried up here someday.

JESS: Ya will?

RACHEL: Yeah. You'll be too, won't ya?

[pause]

JESS: Rach?
RACHEL: Yeah?
JESS: Do ya think we'll still be able ta talk ta each other?
RACHEL: When?
JESS: I mean, like we are now.
RACHEL: We'll be dead, stupid.
JESS: I know, I know. I mean...
RACHEL: We won't have nothin new ta talk about when
    we're dead.
JESS: I guess so.
RACHEL: Same as every other day. Same old nothin new ta
    talk about.

[pause]

JESS: Anythin happenin over your place?
RACHEL: The usual world war three. It's like the Day After
    every day.
JESS: How's things with your mom?
RACHEL: Last night she comes at me with my brother's
    hockey stick.
JESS: What happened?
RACHEL: What happened? She calls me a slut, see what
    happens.
JESS: What did ya say after that?
RACHEL: Nervea that callin me a slut. I gave it to her in the
    stomach.
JESS: Ya hit her?
RACHEL: Nervea that callin me a slut. She gives more rides
    than Air Canada.
JESS: Rach, ya shouldn't hit your mom.
RACHEL: I tried to talk reason with her, ya know. Sense
    with her.
JESS: Yeah?
RACHEL: It's a wastea time. She's a fuckin drunk.

10

JESS: So what started it this time?

RACHEL: She said the only reason Craig's comin home is ta make me pregnant.

JESS: So?

RACHEL: So, why does she talk ta me like I'm retarded?

JESS: I don't know.

RACHEL: Am I retarded?

JESS: No.

RACHEL: Not yet anyways. I probly will be someday. Insanity runs in the family.

JESS: Ya know what ya should try an do? Ya should buy her show tickets.

[*pause*]

RACHEL: What the fuck? Did I hear ya?

JESS: Yeah, I saved an got my parent's tickets ta see Roger Whittaker at Centre 200.

RACHEL: What the fuck. Roger Whittaker?

JESS: Yeah, they loved me for that. They never got on my case for months.

RACHEL: Ya make me sick Jess.

JESS: Ya haveta try an get along.

RACHEL: Goody-two shoes. What'd ya ever do so bad ya had ta buy em show tickets?

JESS: That time ya took mom's good silver for the hot knives?

RACHEL: Oh yeah. An I smoked up in your garage. That was awful.

JESS: You were losin it. Remember ya thought my dad's barbecue was grinnin at ya?

RACHEL: Yep. All this time after, an I'm still losin it.

[*pause*]

JESS: Rach. If ya can't patch things up, maybe ya should just move out.

RACHEL: Yeah, Einstein. Where would I go?

JESS: Stay at my house. My folks wouldn't care.
RACHEL: Jess, they hate me. They think I'm a bad influence on ya.
JESS: Maybe we could maybe share an apartment.
RACHEL: I got no fuckin money, Jess. Neither do you. We gonna get a damn condo?

[*pause*]

JESS: I wish I could loan ya some money. If I had it, I would.
RACHEL: Ya wish ya could. I wish I had a pony. Wishes are stupid.
JESS: I'm sorry.
RACHEL: Jess. I didn't mean ta snap at ya.
JESS: That's alright.
RACHEL: You're my buddy always. Ya know that?
JESS: Rach. I'd...do anythin for ya. Anythin I could ever do.
RACHEL: Yeah. I know.

[*CRAIG enters.*]

CRAIG: *(shouting)* G'day clowns!
JESS: Craiggie!
RACHEL: Hey baby, how's it hangin!
CRAIG: Look at it baby, it's more than hangin it's fuckin draggin.
RACHEL: Oh ya wish. Ya wish!
CRAIG: So what's goin on?
RACHEL: This is it. You're lookin at it.
JESS: How ya doin man?
CRAIG: Not so bad Jessie. You gettin a little bald on top.
JESS: *(laughs)* So are you, man.
CRAIG: Hey. It's a signa potency ain't it, Rach.
RACHEL: No it ain't. It's a signa you're losin your fuckin hair.
JESS: So yeah, we heard ya were doin somethin up in Dartmouth.
CRAIG: Yeah, I had a couplea jobs but I fucked off.

RACHEL: That's not too surprisin.

CRAIG: Na, they were shit jobs anyway. They were beneath humans. Even Jessie.

JESS: *(laughs)* Fuck you.

CRAIG: Tell ya what, I got some plans though. I'm gonna raise hell out here.

JESS: Yeah?

CRAIG: Just watch me man. Just fuckin watch me.

RACHEL: Ya haveta stay home causea probation, right?

CRAIG: Yeah. It's just bullshit. They're makin me check in once a week.

RACHEL: Least ya ain't gonna run off on anyone this time.

CRAIG: Oh yeah? I'm gonna do whatever I want. They can't stop me.

JESS: So what do you guys wanna do?

[*pause*]

CRAIG: Let's go get drunk. Youse got any money for partyin?

RACHEL: We're broke. We can't afford the bars.

CRAIG: *(laughs)* I'm probly still banished from most of em anyway.

RACHEL: Ya look good, Craig.

CRAIG: Hey. Ya look good yourself.

RACHEL: Thanks.

CRAIG: Why youse hangin out in the fuckin graveyard?

JESS: Y'know...it's...central. Rach?

RACHEL: Me an Jess used ta play up here when we were little.

CRAIG: Oh yeah, where was I when youse were playin?

JESS: You were probly playin Dan's poker machines over the store.

CRAIG: *(laughs)* Yeah.

JESS: I useda see ya in there before we even hung out.

CRAIG: Ya know once I ran up like twenty thousand credits there, man.

JESS: Fuck off. Did ya?

CRAIG: Oh yeah. But when it came time ta pay out he gypped me hard.

RACHEL: Speakina gettin gypped, guess who ya know that's workin there?

CRAIG: Fuck off. Whattya doin down there?

RACHEL: Playin with myself. Whattya think? I'm workin for a livin.

CRAIG: Workin for Dirty Dan the Candy Man. I don't call that livin.

RACHEL: I don't wanna hear about it. I gotta go back now for a double shift.

JESS: Are ya serious?

RACHEL: Yeah I'm serious. Thinks I got no life.

JESS: What a bastard.

CRAIG: Tell him to fuck off from his old pal Craig.

RACHEL: You got a job for me? I'm gonna meet up with youse after.

CRAIG: You better.

RACHEL: We can get caught up.

CRAIG: Yeah, let's do that.

JESS: Where do you wanna go, Craig?

[*pause*]

CRAIG: May's well go ta Horton's.

JESS: *(laughs)* Where else?

RACHEL: *(exiting)* You guys could walk me downtown if ya were gentlemen.

JESS: *(following)* Sure. Craig?

CRAIG: Yeah. Let's go paint the town.

[*THEY are gone.*]

Scene 2

Outside Dan's Dairy. Late Evening.

[On the step.]

JESS: That's onea my lawns across the street there. What a dive.

CRAIG: Still the old lawn boy, eh?

JESS: That one's putrid. I almost got bit by a rat there last year.

RACHEL: Ya want ta know what I found there one time when I was walkin home?

JESS: What?

RACHEL: A cat's paw. Cut off.

JESS: Oh, sick.

RACHEL: A cut off cat's paw, right in the front yard by the sidewalk.

JESS: Whose cat was it?

RACHEL: The fuck would I know, Jess. The resta the cat wasn't attached.

CRAIG: (*laughs*) Jess finally got some pussy with his lawnmower.

JESS: I think I woulda noticed somethin like that.

RACHEL: This neighborhood is just a sewer. It doesn't need a fuckin gardener.

JESS: I practically run the whole business now, Craig.

RACHEL: He's still always broke.

JESS: Fuck you.

RACHEL: I hate this job. I hate it.

CRAIG: Yeah?

RACHEL: Yeah. Being cooped up in this little place with Dan ain't my idea of a hot time.

CRAIG: He must be fuckin ancient now.

JESS: Yeah. An he's bein real cheap to her.

CRAIG: Ya makin any money?

RACHEL: Oh yeah. Wheelbarrows full of it.

15

JESS: She really hates her job.

[*RACHEL lights up.*]

RACHEL: Ya know what's the worst? I ask for a tiny raise
    he says he's got no money.
CRAIG: Yeah?
RACHEL: It's bullshit. I know he got the money. An he got
    plenty ta spare.
CRAIG: How do ya know that?
RACHEL: He's got this safe in the back room out where the
    videos are.
CRAIG: He couldn't makin that much money, he needs a
    safe.
RACHEL: No? I seen him open it the other day an I saw him
    countin the money.
JESS: How much was it?
RACHEL: I just kinda for curiousity looked over his shoul-
    der at his count sheet.
CRAIG: How much did it say?
RACHEL: It said forty thousand dollars.

[*pause*]

CRAIG: No shit. You gotta be kiddin.
RACHEL: Isn't that disgusting?
JESS: He must be doin good.
RACHEL: Doin good. Minimum wage, Jess. I'm makin
    mininum fuckin wage.
CRAIG: This little dinky store.
RACHEL: I'm makin fuckin bus fare every hour.
JESS: He could afford ta give ya a raise, then.
RACHEL: Damn right he could. He's got forty thousand
    bucks just sittin in there.

[*pause*]

CRAIG: This place is shit. It's just a hole in the wall.

JESS: Yeah, this store can't be takin in that much money.

RACHEL: Jess, you should see how he rips people off. I work here now. I know.

CRAIG: He oughta be careful.

RACHEL: He's not worried with this safe. You should see his safe.

CRAIG: Yeah?

JESS: An Dan he practically lives here in the store. Drinkin his tea.

RACHEL: Oh yeah, he's all the time askin ya questions.

JESS: He says all his family's moved out west.

RACHEL: Rachel, how's your love life? Rachel, ya got a boyfriend? Rachel this, that...

JESS: He always wants ta know everythin goin on.

RACHEL: I wouldn't even mind talkin to him but he's fuckin deaf.

CRAIG: He stays here all night, eh?

RACHEL: Right till close every night. Hangin over your friggin shoulder.

JESS: He's a real lonely case.

RACHEL: If an I catch him talkin ta me over onea those magazines again, that's it.

JESS: Remember the magazines?

CRAIG: Oh yeah. There was some twisted shit on those racks.

JESS: *(laughing)* What was the animal one?

CRAIG: Yeah, Yeah..."My Four-Legged Lover."

JESS: Yeah. That's it. Yeah, he still got that one.

CRAIG: *(chants)* Bestiality's best, boys. Bestiality's best...

RACHEL: You guys are demented.

JESS: I don't think he even knows whats in em, Rach.

CRAIG: It's about this vet. This gorgeous fuckin vet...

RACHEL: I don't wanna hear about it, Craig!

CRAIG: ...And she like, goes down on dogs. Fuckin collies, beagles. It's incredible.

JESS: Did ya read it?

[pause]

CRAIG: What the fuck. Are ya stupid? Of course I didn't
  read it.
RACHEL: Oh yeah?
CRAIG: I mean I maybe looked through it. For a laugh.
  Y'know, I didn't like...
JESS: Sure ya didn't. Sure!
RACHEL: Craig, you got a sick mind, baby. We never knew...
CRAIG: Fuck you, Lawnboy!

[CRAIG shoves him.]

JESS: *(laughs)* Who'd ever buy that shit around here
  anyways?
RACHEL: Ya'd be suprised. He makes money corruptin
  people. What is that?
JESS: Jeez.
RACHEL: Well I gotta go in now an be a bitch. I'll see youse
  at Horton's then?
JESS: Twelve-thirtyish?
RACHEL: Wha?
CRAIG: Forty thousand bucks. Ya seen him count it?
RACHEL: Yeah. I saw the sheet. An he said it was a bad
  week. Imagine.
JESS: I wish I had bad weeks like that.
RACHEL: Someone smoke the resta this. I gotta go in now
  or he'll freak.

[SHE goes inside.]

CRAIG: Dirty Dan...
JESS: Where'd he get all that money anyway?
CRAIG: From rippin off wads like you, Lawnboy.
JESS: Dan the Man.
CRAIG: Eats his dinner from a garbage can.

JESS: She been there two years an he won't even pay her over minimum wage.

CRAIG: "Oh Danny boy...Ooohh Danny boy...the pipes...the pipes are callin..."

JESS: "I loovve you so..."

CRAIG: So what do ya wanna do now?

[*pause*]

JESS: I don't know. What do you wanna do?

CRAIG: I don't know Jess. Maybe that's why I asked you.

JESS: Sounds good ta me.

CRAIG: You been inhalin fuckin lawnmower fumes or what?

JESS: *(laughs)* Aw, fuck off Craig.

CRAIG: Hey. Let's go find some poker machines. Score some coin.

JESS: Yeah. We could go back an hang out with Rach.

CRAIG: Na. I ain't gonna play poker on those machines. No way.

JESS: Why?

[*pause*]

CRAIG: They're *rigged*, that's why. The old fucker's got the games rigged.

JESS: Yeah?

CRAIG: Yeah. Ya can't beat them. He never pays out. That's why he never pays out.

JESS: He shouldn't be able ta get away with that.

CRAIG: No one can beat a rigged game. No matter how good ya are.

[*They exit.*]

SCENE 3
Inside Tim Horton's, Charlotte Street. Late Night.

[*RACHEL has just arrived.*]

RACHEL: I'm just savin enough for my camaro. That's how I'm copin with it.

CRAIG: Yeah?

RACHEL: An then I'm gonna drive it right through his plate glass window.

CRAIG: Good plan.

RACHEL: I'm really startin ta hate Horton's. Oh God, look at that guy.

CRAIG: What guy?

RACHEL: *(to MAN)* Excuse me. Do ya have ta fuckin wear your chili?

CRAIG: Oh, gross me out, there's beans in his fuckin beard!

RACHEL: No wonder people go retarded when ya gotta hang out with retards.

[*pause*]

CRAIG: Hard night at Danny Boy's?

RACHEL: Tell me about it. Five hours. Five-fifteen an hour. What a waste.

CRAIG: Ya know what's a waste? All that money sittin in that safea his.

RACHEL: *(laughs)* Me an Jess were rememberin the shopliftin game.

CRAIG: If I went back in now, I'd get more than his fuckin hearing aid.

RACHEL: Oh yeah? What would ya get? Me?

CRAIG: Yeah. But then, I'd haveta get enough money ta afford ya.

RACHEL: I wouldn't worry. I'm goin cheap these days.

CRAIG: So, I'd haveta get his safe too. Want me ta get it for ya?

RACHEL: Sure. You're never borin, Craig, ya know that?

[*JESS arrives with coffee.*]

RACHEL: Oh, thanks Jessie. I'm gonna pay ya back, kay?

JESS: Sure. Whenever.

CRAIG: What are you, her four legged lover or somethin?

RACHEL: It's worse. He's got movies now. Move the ashtray over.

JESS: You should see his movies.

RACHEL: It's disgusting. An people rent these things. Our neighbors.

CRAIG: I bet you love lookin at those movies, Rach.

RACHEL: I work for a pervert an that's what it is. Little kids come in there.

CRAIG: That's where he's makin all his bucks. On jerk-offs like my stepfather.

RACHEL: Speakina perverts, ya didn't hear about John MacCormick, did ya?

JESS: Mister McCormick. Our old social studies teacher?

RACHEL: He just got busted on like 15 counts of child sexual abuse.

CRAIG: Yeah?

JESS: Yeah. It just happened last week, they arrested him at school.

RACHEL: He was such a good guy. An this was happenin. No one knew.

CRAIG: Hands-on John!

RACHEL: He was Jessie's favorite teacher. Wasn't he?

JESS: He never hurt me any.

RACHEL: Yeah, I don't know if I believe it. He wouldn't hurt a fly, I think.

CRAIG: Yeah. He'd probably love a fuckin fly. He'd probly love your fly.

21

[*pause*]

JESS: It's hard ta believe.

CRAIG: *(laughs)* They get him behind bars, the other inmates'll probly torture him.

JESS: I guess there's a lotta perverts in our neighborhood.

[*pause*]

RACHEL: *(sings)* "These are the perverts in your neighborhood..."

CRAIG: *(joining)* "...In your neighorhood..."

JESS: *(trio)* "...In your neigh-bor-hood...Yes...these are the perverts in..."

RACHEL: "In your neigh-bor-hood, oh..."

JESS: The security guard is lookin at us.

CRAIG: Let him look.

RACHEL: Hey! What are ya lookin at anyways?

JESS: Rach. He'll kick us out...

RACHEL: We're allowed ta sing. There's no rules here against singin, are there?

JESS: Hey, Mister McCormick wasn't as bad as Mister MacPhee.

RACHEL: Yeah. MacPhee usedta pick his nose and wipe it on the World Globe.

CRAIG: Mrs. Lewis usedta pick her nose too.

RACHEL: *(laughing)* No, she didn't. Did she? You're breakin my heart.

CRAIG: Yeah, you shoulda seen inside her desk. It was a fuckin booger museum.

JESS: She's dyin now.

[*pause*]

RACHEL: Yeah. I heard she got cancer. Fuckin everyone around here got cancer.

JESS: They say it's somethin in the water.

22

RACHEL: You're damn right it's in the water. They lie to us about what's in the water.

JESS: It's probly in the coffee too.

RACHEL: Now there's a cheery thought, Jess. Thanks for that.

JESS: Sorry.

RACHEL: I usedta think this place was so safe y'know. Have kids. Now...

JESS: What?

RACHEL: Who wants ta have kids when they have ta grow up in a dump?

JESS: I don't know. It's home...

[*pause*]

RACHEL: That's why ya need a car. Ya got a car. Ya can take off if ya want.

CRAIG: Maybe you can get your car sooner than ya think.

RACHEL: At this rate I'm savin, I doubt it.

CRAIG: Ya never know. Anythin can happen.

JESS: Yeah. Ya could win one.

RACHEL: Jess. I can't even win a fuckin day old muffin.

JESS: If ya keep tryin though, someday it might pay off.

RACHEL: I know. By the time I can afford the car, I'll have cancer like everyone else in town.

JESS: We better get outta here, the security guard keeps lookin at us.

RACHEL: What, we're not doin nothin!

CRAIG: Fuck him.

RACHEL: *(shouting)* Hey buddy, take a fuckin photograph!

JESS: Relax. I'll get ya another coffee.

CRAIG: Get me one too will ya, I'll pay ya back.

JESS: Sure ya will. Outta that fortune we made on the poker machines?

CRAIG: Don't ya worry, Jess. I always pay back. You know me.

JESS: Maybe I'll just sit down again till the line thins out.

RACHEL: Sure, whatever ya wanna do Jess.

CRAIG: Sure. Whatever ya wanna do.

[*pause*]

JESS: I'm gonna...go to the bathroom. Do ya want anythin else?

RACHEL: From the bathroom?

CRAIG: Give the security guy a shot in the head for me.

JESS: *(laughs)* Yeah, right.

[*HE goes.*]

RACHEL: I thought this was a free country.

CRAIG: What the fuck ever gave ya that idea?

RACHEL: Fuckin 20 minute time limit. What are ya supposed ta do, go home?

CRAIG: No one's gonna force us out if we don't feel like it.

RACHEL: I just hate people lookin at me like I'm shit.

CRAIG: We are shit. We're broke. That means we're shit.

RACHEL: Thanks. You're a big help.

CRAIG: It don't mean nothin. It just means we gotta make some money.

RACHEL: You gonna try an get a job now you're home?

CRAIG: *(laughs)* Oh, that's a good one. Where?

RACHEL: Ya know over behind K-mart, the miniature golf?

CRAIG: Yeah.

RACHEL: Jess mows the lawn there. He says they're lookin for someone ta work.

CRAIG: Miniature golf pro. Oh boy.

RACHEL: No, it's for the chipwagon.

CRAIG: Oh, wouldn't that be a fuckin fun time.

RACHEL: I know. But ya gotta survive somehow, don't ya?

[*pause*]

CRAIG: Hey Rach.

RACHEL: Yeah?

CRAIG: Do ya get a lotta cops drivin by the store at night?

RACHEL: Na. Not really. Why?

CRAIG: Just wonderin.

RACHEL: Craig?

CRAIG: What?

RACHEL: *(laughs)* Go on...

CRAIG: Just thinka the money. Just thinka the potential.

RACHEL: Ya shouldn't be talkin about this here. Someone might think you're serious.

CRAIG: I am serious. I'm dead serious.

RACHEL: Ya are. So why you tellin me about this?

CRAIG: Cause you're parta the plan.

RACHEL: I am. How? What plan? What are ya talkin about?

CRAIG: I know how we could do it. I been thinkin ever since ya told me.

RACHEL: *(laughs)* Oh come off it, Craig. You're too funny.

CRAIG: I'm not jokin around here. Think about it.

[pause]

RACHEL: I can't say I never thought about it. But...

CRAIG: Do ya believe in fate? Do ya believe in fate and the stars an shit?

RACHEL: So what if I do?

CRAIG: Listen. This is fate. Somethin makes ya go look over Dan's shoulder...

RACHEL: That's fate.

CRAIG: Yeah. Ya see forty thousand bucks on the sheet...

RACHEL: Craig. It ain't like we could ever do somethin like that.

CRAIG: Hold on. A few days later, some Judge tells me go home serve my probation...

RACHEL: You're supposedta stay outta trouble, aren't ya?

CRAIG: Sure I am. So there you are with the knowledge, here I am with expertise.

RACHEL: Oh, you're an expert? Since when?

CRAIG: I know how ta do it. And there's our dear old friend Dan Dan.

RACHEL: It's pretty temptin. It is. Ya haveta admit.

[pause]

CRAIG: But, we'd haveta do it soon. Really soon. We gotta
    jump on this.
RACHEL: Hold your horses, will ya? I never said I was doin it.
CRAIG: He's gonna take the money to a bank or somethin.
    He must deposit...
RACHEL: I don't know. I just count the float. Craig?
CRAIG: Can ya get hold of a car somewheres?
RACHEL: What? Ya mean like a 'getaway' car?
CRAIG: I'm not tryin ta be funny here. We need a car.
RACHEL: Obviously I couldn't get a car. If I'm ever drivin
    it's in Jessie's mom's car.
CRAIG: I wouldn't want Jessie in on this.
RACHEL: Why?
CRAIG: Cause. He's your friend, he's my friend. But he's a
    fuck up. He's burnt.
RACHEL: Poor Jess. He's got a good heart, though.
CRAIG: What a fuckin chance we got. It'll be so easy...

[pause]

RACHEL: I really gotta think...
CRAIG: Ya better think fast. Any day now, that money could
    be goin to a bank.
RACHEL: Jessie's comin. Shh...
CRAIG: Forty fuckin grand buys a shitload of day old muf-
    fins.
RACHEL: I know, I know.

[JESSIE returns with more coffee.]

CRAIG: Let's get outta this place. I'm gonna walk ya home.
JESS: Hey...
CRAIG: Some lineup, eh?
JESS: Yeah. Service here sucks. Did I tell ya I wrote a letter
    about it?

RACHEL: Really? Ya wrote ta Tim Horton's?

JESS: Yeah, I wrote ta Tim Horton in Ontario about the bad service at this location.

[*pause*]

CRAIG: Wait a second. Wait a second. You wrote ta Tim Horton?

JESS: Yeah. So?

CRAIG: You're one in a million, buddy.

RACHEL: Did ya say at the top...Dear Mr. Horton?

JESS: Yeah. So?

[*THEY bust up laughing.*]

RACHEL: Earth ta Jessie. Come in!

CRAIG: He's dead, you bone! He was a hockey player!

RACHEL: Didn't ya ever look at the picture on the wall?

JESS: I thought that was Daryl Sittler.

RACHEL: Gotta love ya, Jess. Slooowwwww Learnnnner.

JESS: *(laughs)* Oh you guys fuck off, will ya?

RACHEL: Hey Jess, who were ya callin?

JESS: No one. I had ta call home.

CRAIG: They waitin up for ya?

JESS: Oh yeah. They got no lives.

RACHEL: If they love ya Jess, you're lucky they give a shit that much.

CRAIG: *(laughs)* Yeah, Jess. Maybe you should head home.

RACHEL: Yeah. If they're worried about ya.

JESS: They're not worried about me. I'm gonna walk you home.

RACHEL: Oh, you don't have ta do that.

JESS: I don't mind. I always walk ya home.

RACHEL: Craig?

[*pause*]

JESS: Yeah. Maybe I should head home.

RACHEL: I'll be alright.

JESS: That's good.

CRAIG: Do ya think ya could get your old lady's car some night this week?

JESS: I don't know. Probly. What for?

RACHEL: I got the day after tomorrow off. Why don't we try an get a gamea pool?

JESS: All right. Good seein ya, Craig.

CRAIG: Smell ya later, my four legged friend.

JESS: *(laughs)* Not if I smell ya first.

RACHEL: See ya Jess.

JESS: Get home safe.

[*JESS exits.*]

SCENE *4*

A billiard hall. Evening.

[*Playing pool.*]

JESS: YES. IN THERE.

RACHEL: WE'RE STARTIN A COMEBACK.

CRAIG: Oh yeah? Well, I'm just warmin up, kiddies.

RACHEL: Uh oh. I think we made him mad.

CRAIG: Ya musta got lotsa practice while I was gone off makin my own way.

JESS: It was a lucky shot, Craig.

RACHEL: It wasn't a lucky shot. Jess, ya can't go givin in all the time.

CRAIG: Hey, whose side are you on anyway?

RACHEL: I'm on whosever side I wanna be on. I like the underdog.

CRAIG: Underdog-shit. I know how ya like bein on top.

RACHEL: *(laughs)* Just take the shot, will ya. We're runnin outta time.

CRAIG: Chalk this up. Six in the side.

JESS: If ya get this one in, I know you're hustlin me.

CRAIG: Oh, ya wanna put some money on it, Jess?

JESS: No thanks.

RACHEL: I'll bet ya a loonie ya don't even come close ta the six.

CRAIG: A whole loonie? Hey, don't break the bank, Rach.

[*CRAIG shoots.*]

RACHEL: That is the bank an...that's what ya get for bein a smartass.

JESS: This is it. Eight ball corner pocket.

CRAIG: Go for it Jess.

[*pause*]

RACHEL: In this lifetime Jess, alright? We can't afford another hour.

JESS: Alright, alright.

CRAIG: Line it up Jess, you're not launchin the fuckin space shuttle here.

JESS: Hey. I can win with this shot.

CRAIG: But you're not gonna win. You're gonna choke. Ya always choke.

JESS: Yeah, wanna bet? This shot's easy. A little kid could make it.

CRAIG: Now you're talkin, Jess. Let's bet.

RACHEL: Craig, if Jess misses it, I'll blow everyone in this pool hall.

JESS: Rach. I don't need that kinda pressure, okay?

CRAIG: Na, I don't wanna bet that.

RACHEL: I won't have ta do it, Jessie. I know you're gonna make it.

CRAIG: She already blew mosta them anyway.
RACHEL: *(hits him)* You better be nice to me, buddy. I know too much.

[*CRAIG stops the game.*]

CRAIG: *(takes out wallet)* I'll bet ya a thousand bucks ya miss.
RACHEL: Ya right. We're on Fantasy Island now.
JESS: Sure. Why don't we just bet a million?
CRAIG: Come on Lawnboy. How bout two thousand? I can pay ya next week.
RACHEL: He ain't serious, Jess.
CRAIG: The fuck I am. I never kid about money. Do I, Jess?
JESS: Okay. What's the joke?
CRAIG: No joke. If ya make the shot, I'll give ya the money this weekend.
RACHEL: Sure ya will. An the Pope's gonna turn Mormon. Forget it Jess...
JESS: Craig. We had ta scrape for enough for the table for an hour.
CRAIG: I'm gonna have over ten thousand bucks. This Sunday.

[*pause*]

RACHEL: Craig. Are ya outta your fuckin mind?
CRAIG: An ya know what? Even if I lost the game I'd still have enough..
RACHEL: Ya think you're gonna do it this weekend?
CRAIG: For a prelude. Onea those nice little neons. A camaro. Anythin I want.
RACHEL: I thought ya said ya weren't gonna talk about this with him...
CRAIG: It's okay. I know what I'm doin.
RACHEL: Craig. Ya never said anythin about this weekend.
JESS: What is he sayin?

CRAIG: We need a car. I ain't gonna find anyone else on short notice.

RACHEL: Craig. I'm not decided if I'm in this yet.

JESS: What's goin on? What're ya whisperin about?

RACHEL: He's talkin...about the store, Jess.

JESS: What about the store?

CRAIG: Take your shot, Jess.

JESS: I don't wanna shoot. I wanna hear about the store.

[*pause*]

CRAIG: If I was ta ever look at a dream set up. A fuckin dreamy set up.

RACHEL: My store.

CRAIG: Your store. Your store. Huh? Do you own like shares of stock in it?

RACHEL: Ya shouldn't keep talkin about this in public places.

CRAIG: They don't know what we're talkin about. People are basically stupid.

JESS: Okay. I get it. This is about..the store. Right?

CRAIG: Jess. It's all in there. It's *waitin* for us.

JESS: Us?

CRAIG: Yeah Jess. I'm givin ya a chance ta get in on it with us. Go three ways.

[*pause*]

JESS: Rach?

RACHEL: Craig. This is way too fast.

CRAIG: I told ya, that's why it's perfect. Cause it is fast. Besides, it has ta be fast.

RACHEL: Well, you're goin too fast for me. This ain't professional.

CRAIG: Oh, so now you're the expert on what's professional, are ya?

RACHEL: Do it yourself if you're gonna do it. I'm out of it.

31

[pause]

CRAIG: Ya know what Rach? Ya make me sick to my stomach sometimes.

RACHEL: How, Craig? How do I make ya sick to your stomach?

CRAIG: With your talk. Talk is fuckin cheap.

RACHEL: What talk is cheap? I never said anythin.

CRAIG: You know what talk. Maybe all you can do is talk.

JESS: I'm gonna take my shot now.

RACHEL: You don't know what you're talkin about, Craig!

CRAIG: Maybe all you got is a good mouth!

RACHEL: You're crazy if ya think that about me.

CRAIG: I got no this, that. I got no life. I got no future. Ya act so fuckin tough.

JESS: Eight ball in the side pocket.

CRAIG: Someone comes up ta ya with a real opportunity, ya think he's crazy.

RACHEL: It is crazy. We ain't gonna rob Dan's Dairy. We grew up with that store.

JESS: Rach...

CRAIG: It ain't crazy. You're crazy. You just ain't got the guts for it.

RACHEL: So what are ya sayin? You're sayin I'm chickenshit?

CRAIG: Ya want it. Ya want it but you're too weak ta take it!

RACHEL: I'm leavin. This is a wastea my time.

CRAIG: Yeah? Ya say I'm wastin your time? You're a waste!

RACHEL: Ya think so, do ya?

CRAIG: Yeah. I think so. You are raw fuckin waste. An you're a wastea my time.

JESS: Hey man, calm down okay?

CRAIG: I'm calm. I'm just sayin. When ya got a chance at real money.

JESS: You're talkin about...what I think you're talkin about. Aren't ya?

CRAIG: Life is short, Jess. No one gives ya anythin good. Ya haveta go an take it before someone else does.

[*pause*]

JESS: I know. But...you're talkin about...a robbery of Dan's.
CRAIG: Sure it is. Great or small, Jess. Great or fuckin small.
JESS: What do ya mean? Dan is...He...likes me. Sometimes...
CRAIG: I bet he loves ya. Ya said yourself ya get ripped off every day in there.
JESS: Craig. He's...old. He usedta be really nice to us. Remember?
CRAIG: He got rich off us! All these years. Pretendin like he's our fuckin grandpa!

[*pause*]

JESS: Rach?
RACHEL: I know what gettin ripped off is.
CRAIG: Hey. We were fuckin born ripped off. There's right and wrong.
RACHEL: That's my store. I been goin up ta that store since I was little.
CRAIG: Dirty Dan, the Porno Man. Oh, I didn't know ya loved the guy.
RACHEL: No, Craig. I don't love the guy. An I don't like gettin ripped off either.
CRAIG: So what, Rach? Ya gonna get sentimental or are ya gonna get in?

[*pause*]

RACHEL: I ain't talkin here. Let's go somewhere else away from people.
CRAIG: I gotta tell ya about the new plan. It's even better than the last one. It's foolproof.
RACHEL: It better be if Jess is in it.

CRAIG: Jess?

[*pause*]

JESS: I took my last shot. When no one was lookin.
CRAIG: What happened?
JESS: I missed. I scratched. On the eight ball. I guess...I lose.
RACHEL: Hey. It's alright.
JESS: I choked. I always choke, don't I? Why?
CRAIG: Come on for a little walk with us, Jessie.

[*pause*]

JESS: Where we goin?
RACHEL: We haveta find someplace where there's no people.
Where there's not a soul.

[*THEY exit.*]

[*JESS follows.*]

Scene 5
The Grounds of The Steel Plant. On a Bridge.

[*Throwing rocks at a streetlamp.*]

RACHEL: When I was little, I usedta think there was a mon-
ster in the tarpond.
JESS: My mom, she told me they usedta swim out in the
harbour.
RACHEL: Yeah, sure. Sydney Harbour? Swimmin? I'll bet.
JESS: Yeah. She told me when they were little. Over by the
Yacht Club.

34

CRAIG: Your mama swam in the harbour. That explains a lot, Jess.

RACHEL: If ya fell in that stuff, no one'd ever know. It'd just swallow ya.

JESS: Yeah. I guess they wouldn't.

RACHEL: I bet...no one'd even bother ta look for ya in that shit.

CRAIG: Nope. Ya wouldn't have a prayer.

[*pause*]

RACHEL: Jess? What would ya do if ya had forty thousand dollars?

JESS: I never thought much about it.

RACHEL: C'mon, buddy. Everyone thinks about it.

CRAIG: What would you do with it?

RACHEL: Ninety-two fuel injected six cylinder Alpine stereo, say no more.

CRAIG: Yeahhh.

RACHEL: A guy's sellin it up on Green Road he only wants fifty-five hundred.

CRAIG: Chicken feed.

RACHEL: It ain't chicken feed when you're savin like, thirty dollars a month.

CRAIG: Alright, Jess. Enough's enough. What are ya thinkin?

JESS: About what?

CRAIG: About what. About the store. Whattya think? I explained the plan.

RACHEL: Craig's got a good plan, Jess. It's a really good plan.

CRAIG: It'll be like lightning. He won't know what hit him.

RACHEL: He couldn't connect it with you or me in a million years.

JESS: I don't know about all this.

CRAIG: Well what the fuck don't ya know? I explained it back ta front.

[*pause*]

JESS: We...buy things there.

CRAIG: Oh fuck. All aboard the idiot train...

RACHEL: Jess, he's an asshole. I got no sympathy for the guy.

CRAIG: Are you on the fuckin dope or somethin? Ya buy things there.

RACHEL: It's forty thousand dollars Jess. I know, at first, it seems impossible.

JESS: It's our store. That's where we go...ta hang out some days.

RACHEL: It is our store. An that's why we should be the ones ta go for it.

JESS: Rach, I could use the money too, but...

CRAIG: But what?

JESS: He never done nothin to me. He's usually sorta friendly to me.

RACHEL: He's a moody fuckin pervert, Jess. You seen the way he looks at me?

JESS: I know he's probly a pervert. But you kinda flirt with him, Rach...

RACHEL: He's a crook too. He wouldn't even pay me minimum wage if he didn't haveta.

CRAIG: It's like I told ya, Jess. He never pays out. Never.

JESS: He never pays out.

CRAIG: Is that fair? Everything's fuckin rigged?

RACHEL: Think about it, Jess. How easy it'll be.

[*pause*]

JESS: I know Dan is a real bastard an everythin. But...he...

RACHEL: What? What are ya tryin ta say?

JESS: There's a sign in the store. Ya know? It says "no loitering."

CRAIG: Where the hell is he goin with this?

JESS: He...lets me. Y'know?

CRAIG: Let you. What does he *let* you, Jess?

36

JESS: Just...he lets me...loiter. Just hang around with Rach. He...lets me.

CRAIG: Fuck off. Just fuck off. I'll walk home after...

RACHEL: Craig, ya can't walk home after. Don't be foolish.

CRAIG: I'm gonna be foolish if I have ta stay up all night with burn-out here.

JESS: He lets me loiter. He never done nothin ta me.

RACHEL: Listen to me. He's only nice to us when we got money ta spend.

JESS: I think I might be doin somethin this Saturday anyway.

CRAIG: What are ya gonna be doin, Jess? Mowin a lawn maybe?

JESS: My father wants me ta paint a fence...for my grand-mother.

RACHEL: There's no problem, then. This is gonna happen at night. After close.

[*pause*]

JESS: Why do you guys want me?

CRAIG: Huh?

JESS: Ya could ask anyone.

RACHEL: We want ya cause you're our friend, Jess.

JESS: Yeah?

CRAIG: Yeah. An we know ya won't blab it all over Cape Breton, will ya?

JESS: No, I won't ever talk about this.

RACHEL: Okay Jessie? I want us ta make some money together.

CRAIG: An all ya have ta do is drive, Jess. That's it.

[*pause*]

JESS: I usedta go in there...an Dan let me read comics all day for free.

RACHEL: Member when we usedta trade Archies? Hey, you still got a buncha mine.

JESS: You still got a buncha my mine, too. All my X-Men.

CRAIG: Hey. Hey. Can we get past the fuckin kidstuff? This ain't professional.

RACHEL: He was nicer to us when we were kids. I remember, too.

[*pause*]

JESS: What if ya got there an the money was already in the safe?

CRAIG: I told ya. I go in there. I say 'open the safe.'

RACHEL: He might not open the safe. Just like that.

JESS: What if he wouldn't open the safe? What if he just...wouldn't?

CRAIG: Don't worry. He'll open the safe.

JESS: How?

CRAIG: Don't worry about it.

JESS: How though?

CRAIG: He'll open the fuckin safe. That I promise you. This time, he'll pay out.

[*pause*]

JESS: What? Are ya gonna have...?

CRAIG: What?

JESS: A...weapon. Like a gun or somethin?

CRAIG: Somethin.

JESS: Yeah? Like a real gun?

CRAIG: Yeah. Ya think they only got them on t.v. or somethin?

JESS: I never seen one up close before.

CRAIG: It'll probly be a knife, though. Gun's too loud. It might wake people.

RACHEL: Dan'd wet his pants if someone came in with a knife.

CRAIG: He'll do what I say. I ain't messin around in there.

RACHEL: He says no'd ever try ta rob him. He thinks he knows everyone in town.

CRAIG: Well he ain't seen me in a long time.

JESS: What if someone gets hurt?

RACHEL: Craig, ya said no one's gonna get hurt.

CRAIG: What did I say? No one's gonna get hurt. Don't worry.

RACHEL: Forty thousand bucks'll be plentya hurt.

JESS: Rach, do they got any hidden cameras there?

RACHEL: Nope.

JESS: No cameras.

RACHEL: He doesn't want ta waste the money, cause he's always there anyway.

CRAIG: He must be the last store on the fuckin planet without cameras.

[pause]

RACHEL: One thirda forty thousand is how much..?

CRAIG: About thirteen grand. An change.

RACHEL: Thirteen thousand dollars. Thirteen thousand dollars.

JESS: Ya never done this before though, did ya Craig?

CRAIG: I done a couplea B an E's. I told ya before. I know exactly how ta do it.

JESS: Ya never done somethin like this though. A robbery.

CRAIG: Jess. I usedta live there playin poker. I know that store inside out.

RACHEL: Jessie. I know it's fast. But sometimes a chance only comes along...

JESS: Rach...it's too fast. It's only the day after tomorrow. I can't...

RACHEL: The quicker it happens. The quicker we got the money. Right?

JESS: You guys could do it without me, y'know? Ya don't need me.

[pause]

RACHEL: Jessie. We do. The thing of it is. We really need your car.

JESS: My car. Ya mean...my mom's car?

RACHEL: But, I also want ya ta be with me Jess. Okay?

JESS: Ya can't use my mom's car for this. That's...outta the question!

RACHEL: You can get it, Jess. I know ya can. All ya gotta do is ask her.

[pause]

CRAIG: It's thirteen grand, ya clown. Flash that wad.

RACHEL: Ya can start all over if ya want. Ya can get some nice clothes.

CRAIG: You'll have women crawlin all over ya. Say g'bye ta Lawnboy.

JESS: Yeah? No they wouldn't. Would they?

RACHEL: Ya can be the nicest person in the world. But ya gotta have money too.

CRAIG: An all ya haveta do is get a car. An drive the car.

RACHEL: Yeah. That's all. You'll be an equal partner.

CRAIG: Ya drop me off. Sit for a bit. Pick me up. Like any other night.

JESS: All I'd have ta do is drive the car? I wouldn't haveta go inside.

RACHEL: It's like gettin paid thirteen thousand bucks for a taxi ride, Jess.

JESS: What if we get caught? What'll happen to us?

CRAIG: We won't get caught. Don't worry.

RACHEL: Jess. It's only in the movies that they always get caught.

JESS: Rach. Me an you got jobs.

RACHEL: No we don't. We got shit jobs. We got slave jobs. Don't kid yourself.

CRAIG: Listen ta Lawnboy with his upwardly mobile position.

JESS: It's gonna be...my business. My dad told me...

CRAIG: You're chokin, Jess! Ya want to be a loser your whole life?

JESS: Couldn't we...maybe go somewheres else. Than Dan's?

CRAIG: No! There's no where else! We know there's money there. It's Dan, an that's final.

[*pause*]

RACHEL: Jessie? Do ya remember the other day, we were up in the graveyard?

JESS: Yeah.

RACHEL: Ya said. If ya had the money ta help me move, ya'd loan it ta me.

JESS: Yeah?

RACHEL: Well, if ya still want ta do somethin nice for me, this is somethin I need.

[*SHE kisses him.*]

JESS: Do ya...really? Do ya need it, Rach?

RACHEL: I'm sicka dreamin things that aren't gonna happen. Aren't you?

CRAIG: It's just sittin there. It's fuckin beggin.

[*pause*]

JESS: Okay. I'll try...an get the car.

[*pause*]

CRAIG: Jess. You're slower than the second cominga Christ, but I love ya anyway!

RACHEL: What made ya change your mind?

JESS: I don't know. I need somethin too.

CRAIG: Can ya get the car for a test drive tomorrow?

JESS: I'll try...I can't...guarantee.

RACHEL: Ya can do it, Jess. I know ya can.

[*JESS fires rocks at the lights, in a fury.*]

JESS: I'm sick! I'm fuckin sick! I'm fuckin sick! I'm fuckin
    sick! I'm fuckin sick!
RACHEL: Jess?
CRAIG: It's already done. We're gonna be rich!
JESS: I need somethin.
CRAIG: It's gonna happen. It's gonna fuckin happen...!
RACHEL: It's in the stars for us...!

[*pause*]

CRAIG: Hey clown...ya got it.
JESS: I did?
RACHEL: Way ta go, Jessie!
CRAIG: Watch the light go out!
JESS: I got it.

[*The light flickers, dims above them. To black.*]

SCENE 6
Outskirts of Sydney. Night.

[*Driving.*]

RACHEL: *(yelling out the window)* I need a CAR.
CRAIG: *(driving)* Turn it UP.
JESS: Don't blow the speakers.
RACHEL: Jess, we gotta turn it up loud it's Friday night!
CRAIG: The night before Christmas.
RACHEL: *(screams)* I'm gonna get my CAR...my own CAR.
CRAIG: YES.
RACHEL: Cause I need this fuckin WIND...!

CRAIG: How can ya fuckin breathe without it?

RACHEL: *(kisses him)* BABY..I was born ta drive. No more droolin over car lots.

CRAIG: This is life. This is what it's all about, buddy. This is it.

JESS: Just don't push it too hard, Craig, okay? Please?

RACHEL: Jessie, ya havin fun back there?

JESS: Yeah. Could I ask a stupid questiona someone?

CRAIG: Since when do ya ask permission, Jess?

JESS: Where we goin right now?

RACHEL: We could go anywhere. The night's young, baby.

JESS: Craig. What about your voice? What if Dan remembers your voice?

CRAIG: It's all figured out, Jess. Don't worry about it.

RACHEL: He's gonna disguise his voice.

JESS: Oh.

RACHEL: Craig does voices now. Impressions. You should hear him. Do one, Craig.

CRAIG: Na, fuck off.

RACHEL: Please, Craig? Do your Jokey. I love your Jokey.

CRAIG: Alright, I'll do Jokey. "HEY SMURFS. I GOT A WIDDLE SUPWISE FOW YA!"

RACHEL: *(roaring)* That is so funny. Okay, now do your Exorcist voice. Please?

CRAIG: "I'M THE DEVIL. KINDLY REMOVE THESE STRAPS."

JESS: That's...great.

CRAIG: "YOUR MOTHER SUCKS COCKS IN HELL."

JESS: Rach. Ya see that little Virgin Mary statue on the dash?

RACHEL: Yeah?

JESS: Could ya put it in the glove compartment please?

RACHEL: Uh oh. Jessie's got religion!

JESS: It's not me..it's my mother.

CRAIG: How bout we see what this baby can do?

JESS: Uh...

RACHEL: Wait slow down, we're goin by the Cape Breton Hospital!

CRAIG: What're ya doin?

RACHEL: *(ecstatic)* WAKE UP CRAZY PEOPLE.

JESS: Rach, they probly need their rest...

RACHEL: WAKE UP RETARDED PEOPLE! YA DON'T KNOW WHAT YOU'RE MISSIN!

JESS: Guys, could we do somethin or go home okay?

CRAIG: Well, we got the car, where do youse wanna go?

JESS: We could go ta Horton's.

CRAIG: Na, fuck that. We always do that.

RACHEL: Let's drive out the East Bay sandbar, I heard there's a party.

JESS: Ya gotta give me gas money if we go that far.

RACHEL: I don't know. We could...go ta Jasper's for a coffee.

JESS: The waitresses hate us there. We can't afford tips.

CRAIG: You fuckin people are pathetic.

RACHEL: Let's just shoot the drag or somethin.

CRAIG: Yeah right. Shoot the drag in a fuckin K-Car. Whoopee.

JESS: It's my mom's car.

[*pause*]

CRAIG: This is what it is. Ya got money. Ya got somewhere ta go.

RACHEL: We could go anywhere. We got a car.

CRAIG: Yeah, we could go anywhere. But there's nowhere.

RACHEL: Yeah. There's nowhere, is there.

[*Driving.*]

SCENE 7

The Same. A Little Later.

[*CRAIG is turning.*]

JESS: We're headin back ta town?

CRAIG: Yeah.

JESS: That's good. Craig?

CRAIG: What?

JESS: Why'd ya get quiet? Is everythin all right with the car?

RACHEL: Sweetie, ya grip that wheel any harder it's gonna fall off.

CRAIG: *(laughs)* I was just thinkin somethin. About old Danny boy.

JESS: What's so funny?

RACHEL: Yeah. Why're ya bein so weird, ya weirdo?

[*pause*]

CRAIG: I was just thinkin about that day he gypped me outta my credits.

RACHEL: Are you still on that? Well, tomorrow, you're gonna get your money.

CRAIG: Old prick. He got away with it for a long time.

[*CRAIG accelerates.*]

JESS: Craig, be careful around here, there's always speedtraps.

RACHEL: What's buggin ya, anyway?

CRAIG: Twenty thousand credits he owes me. Ya know what that is?

RACHEL: I bet it ain't more than thirteen thousand bucks. Don't worry about it.

45

CRAIG: Woulda paid out about only about two fifty. But it's..the achievement.

JESS: Craig. Ya gotta slow down.

CRAIG: This is before he rigged them...

RACHEL: Craig, that was years an years ago. Who cares?

CRAIG: In fact, I bet I'm the reason he rigged the fuckin games.

RACHEL: Can we stay in our own lane here? We're crossin over.

CRAIG: He wouldn't pay out cause he said I was underage. The fuckin criminal.

RACHEL: Well, we're gonna get him back. It's gonna happen.

CRAIG: Yeah, cause no one burns me like that. I don't forget.

JESS: I think I should maybe take the car home now. Craig?

CRAIG: Five an a half hours I played that game. So he calls up the old man.

RACHEL: *(to J.)* He's not listenin to me, either...

CRAIG: Says your kid's outta control. Tells the old man ta keep me on a leash.

JESS: Craig, we should probly take the car back. I told my mom by eleven.

CRAIG: So the old man, he puts me on a leash in the cellar. A fuckin dog's leash.

[*pause*]

RACHEL: Craig. You wanna pull over have a coffee or somethin?

CRAIG: We don't got time for coffee. We got work ta do.

RACHEL: What work? We already went through the practice. Let's just cruise a bit.

CRAIG: We're doin it tonight. We're goin there right now. Get ready.

[*pause*]

RACHEL: No we're not. We're not goin there right now.

CRAIG: Yes we are. Now everyone listen...

RACHEL: What're ya talkin about? Ya said tomorrow. We planned for tomorrow.

CRAIG: We got no guarantee Jessie can get the car tomorrow. Do we?

JESS: Craig. Ya said we were gonna do it tomorrow night. Saturday night.

CRAIG: I know what I'm doin here. Just let me handle it.

RACHEL: Craig. We know ya know what you're doin. Ya made a great plan. But this is...

CRAIG: Look under my seat Jess. There's some cord in a bag.

JESS: What did ya put under the seat? I didn't say...ya could put stuff...

RACHEL: We gotta wait till Saturday, I'm workin! I'm gonna leave the back door open.

CRAIG: It's forty thousand bucks, Rach. Don't get loose on me, okay?

JESS: This is crazy. We can't do it tonight. We're not ready!

CRAIG: We get there. You go talk to Dan. You get in. You leave the door open..

JESS: Craig. The plan's changed. It's really changed...

CRAIG: I'm around the corner. I get in. When I say, hit the lights, you hit the lights.

RACHEL: I have ta what? I have ta talk to him. I have ta...go inside? Face ta face?

CRAIG: Face ta face. Do ya got the guts for it? Don't choke on me, Rach!

RACHEL: I thought I was just gonna haveta leave the door open an wait in the car.

[CRAIG lashes out.]

CRAIG: CAN YA HANDLE IT, RACH? CAN YA HANDLE IT? STOP FUCKIN ME UP...!

JESS: HEY...

RACHEL: I can handle it, Craig. I can handle anything you got!

[*pause*]

JESS: We can still go home. It's not too late...
CRAIG: No one's goin home. Pass that cord up front.
JESS: You're gonna tie him?
RACHEL: Since when are ya gonna tie him? Why do ya haveta tie him?
CRAIG: Just leave everythin ta me. Don't worry about it.
JESS: Where's your mask at? In your pocket?

[*pause*]

RACHEL: Craig...?

[*The car accelerates.*]

SCENE 9
Inside Dan's Dairy. Past Midnight.

[*The store is wrecked.*]

JESS: Rach?

[*pause*]

JESS: It's me, Rach. It's Jess. Let me in.

[*RACHEL is curled up in the shadows.*]

RACHEL: Jessie?

JESS: Rach, we have ta get out of here now. It's takin too
    long.

[*pause*]

RACHEL: Jessie?
JESS: Open the door, Rach. Let me in before someone sees.

[*SHE opens it.*]

RACHEL: Lock the door. Get back from the window.
JESS: Where's Craig?
RACHEL: He...
JESS: Where's Dan? Did he open the safe? What happened?

[*pause*]

RACHEL: *(cracking)* He sounded...just like a little baby.
JESS: Where is he?
RACHEL: It's bad, Jessie. It's really bad.
JESS: Are they in the back room?
RACHEL: He was...friendly to us. He was...nice to us.
JESS: Craig. This is takin too long. We have ta go now!
RACHEL: He offered us...tea. Can ya believe it?
JESS: We gotta go Rach. We can't wait for him.
RACHEL: He said we were his kids. Why were we doin this?

[*pause*]

JESS: Oh god.
RACHEL: Why'd he say that? We're not his kids. He's a...
JESS: Rach...COME ON.
RACHEL: ...a fuckin bastard. He's just a fuckin bastard...he's..
JESS: Rach...stay out of the window.
RACHEL: Why'd he say that? Why'd he say...?
JESS: I don't know. I don't know why he said that. We got
    no time...

RACHEL: We're not even...kids anymore.

JESS: Rach. We can't wait for him...

RACHEL: He wouldn't open the safe. Craig...was screamin at him...

JESS: We can't wait for Craig. We have to go...

RACHEL: He l-locked the door Jess. He wouldn't let me in.

JESS: What's he doin for all this time?

RACHEL: Craig tied him up. It sounded like...like...

JESS: What? What happened?

RACHEL: ...Like he was...torturin him.

[*pause*]

[*JESS is banging on the door as CRAIG opens it. His shirt is bloody.*]

CRAIG: What the fuck are you doin in here?

RACHEL: What did ya do to him?

JESS: You were takin too long. What happened?

[*pause*]

CRAIG: Dirty old fucker wouldn't part with his precious hard earned money.

RACHEL: Craig, he couldn't hear ya. He lost his hearin aid when ya. He lost his hearin aid when ya smashed him in the face!

JESS: What happened in there?

RACHEL: Where is he? What did ya do to him? I have to see it.

JESS: Rach. Keep quiet!

RACHEL: Did he open the safe?

[*pause*]

CRAIG: Hey Rach. Did ya...ever graduate high school? TELL ME!

JESS: We got no time for this, we have ta get out now.

CRAIG: Did ya ever graduate high school?

RACHEL: Yeah. I graduated high school.

CRAIG: Ya did? Ya graduated high school.

RACHEL: Yeah, I graduated fuckin high school! What are ya sayin? What happened?

CRAIG: I didn't graduate high school, Rach. But I know the fuckin difference...

JESS: Craig...back off!

CRAIG: Between forty thousand...

JESS: BACK OFF.

CRAIG: ...And four hundred followed by a fuckin decimal zero zero.

[pause]

RACHEL: What?

[pause]

JESS: We can't stay here. We haveta...go home now. Okay?

RACHEL: Four...hundred?

JESS: Ya read it wrong.

[pause]

RACHEL: What did ya do ta Dan, Craig? What did ya do to him?

CRAIG: He's in back there. Go say hi if ya want.

[JESS moves into the back room.]

RACHEL: Jessie?

CRAIG: He had it comin.

[HE stumbles out.]

51

RACHEL: Craig. Ya said...no one was gonna get hurt! Ya promised!

CRAIG: Well, he had it comin for a long fuckin time. He owed us. He owed me...

JESS: Don't go back there. Ya can't go back there!

[*JESS kneels and vomits.*]

RACHEL: Ya killed him?

CRAIG: Ya said ya wanted it...professional. I did it...

JESS: We have to get out of here right now. We can't stay!

RACHEL: Ya really killed him?

[*SHE is slipping into shock.*]

CRAIG: You retarded fuckin bitch. I should kill you too. Right now!

JESS: LEAVE HER ALONE!

CRAIG: Ya couldn't buy a rear view mirror for a camaro with your share!

JESS: It doesn't matter anymore, Craig! It doesn't matter...

[*pause*]

CRAIG: It matters ta me, Jess. This is my whole fuckin life...here.

[*HE picks up the money bag.*]

JESS: Rach. We have ta go now. An I mean right now, okay?

RACHEL: I'm sorry, Jessie.

JESS: *(to CRAIG)* What are ya doin? Ya can't stay here.

CRAIG: I'm gonna play one game. For old time's sake.

JESS: We're gonna get caught.

CRAIG: No one's gonna get caught. Don't worry about it.

RACHEL: We're goin up ta the store.

JESS: Rach, we're goin home now...

CRAIG: *(at the machine)* Alright. Double up motherfucker. Give us a king.

RACHEL: We're goin up ta the store.

JESS: Rachel, we're at the store. We're goin home.

CRAIG: *(to himself)* Come on flush. Come on flush. Give us a flush.

[*pause*]

JESS: Craig?

CRAIG: Yeah?

JESS: None of us can get caught. If we get caught for this we're dead.

CRAIG: Na. We won't get caught for this. There's no witnesses.

JESS: Craig...*why*?

CRAIG: Except us. We're...home free. I'd even bet money on it.

[*JESS gives up.*]

JESS: We gotta go through the back room Rach. Out the back door.

CRAIG: ...But not on this game, though. I wouldn't fuckin bet on this game...

JESS: Promise me you'll close your eyes, okay? Please...

CRAIG: Cause this fuckin game is rigged. Completely rigged. Ya can't win.

JESS: ...Promise.

[*CRAIG is still playing, as THEY exit.*]

SCENE 10
Behind Dan's Dairy.

[*RACHEL stumbles.*]

RACHEL: I can't...feel my legs.
JESS: Rach, ya haveta get up. Ya can't sit down.
RACHEL: Where we goin?
JESS: We haveta get back ta the car.

[*pause*]

RACHEL: I didn't know...this was gonna happen.
JESS: We can't sit here an think about it now.
RACHEL: I can't feel my legs, Jess.

[*pause*]

JESS: Please. Just stand up. We'll go one step at a time.
RACHEL: No one saw us, Jess.
JESS: I don't know. I don't think so.
RACHEL: It was like...we were invisible.

[*pause*]

JESS: We didn't...do that in there.
RACHEL: I know. It wasn't us...
JESS: He...went crazy.
RACHEL: We didn't know...
JESS: ...How...could we?

[*silence*]

RACHEL: We just kinda went along...for the ride.
JESS: Yeah...

[*pause*]

RACHEL: Cause...ya need...sometimes...
JESS: Yeah...
RACHEL: Ya need...
JESS: I know...
RACHEL: Ya need...*(pause)* I don't know.
JESS: I know. I know what ya mean.
RACHEL: Ya do...?
JESS: Yeah...I do.

[*silence*]

RACHEL: Jessie. I can't...go home now...after this.

[*SHE is slipping away.*]

JESS: Then we'll go for a drive or somethin. We'll just drive
        somewhere. For awhile.
RACHEL: Up ta the store...
JESS: No. Take my hand, Rach. Take my hand. C'mon...

[*HE helps her to her feet.*]

RACHEL: (*childlike*) Where we goin?

[*THEY are gone.*]

[*In the growing darkness, the sound of a car ignition.*]

Striking. Catching.

Roaring.

Blackout

End

HEARTSPENT AND
BLACK SILENCE

Characters

DWAYNE In his middle 20's.

SHELLY In her early 20's.

Place
The grounds of a harness racing stadium; Tartan
Downs, in Sydney, Nova Scotia.

Time
From early evening, through the night,
to the earlymorning.

The Set
The set demands can be met with a waist high rail,
made of either slatted white wood or rusted chain link.
There is a bench, painted in green and white,
covered with dried pigeon shit and
old bubble gum. Next to the bench is a metal trash can.

Heartspent and Black Silence was first produced at the "On the Waterfront" Festival in Dartmouth, Nova Scotia, on May 4, 1995.

SHELLY Irene Poole

DWAYNE Stephen Hines

The production was directed by Steven Manuel.

SCENE 1

DWAYNE and SHELLY are arriving at the end of a long line-up to get into the races. The sounds of the track are heard in the distance.

SHELLY: I thought we were goin ta the Triple. Why are we comin down the track for?

DWAYNE: This is the suprise. It's gonna be better than movies.

SHELLY: Since when do we ever come down the track? Ya know ya can't gamble.

DWAYNE: How do you know I can't gamble? I know a bit about horse racin.

SHELLY: Dwayne. I had ta explain the Pick-Three lotto to ya five times.

DWAYNE: You're fulla shit, ya did.

SHELLY: Well, I ain't gonna be your date if ya plan on losin your shirt.

DWAYNE: Ya have ta be my date. We're married.

[pause]

SHELLY: I guess the track's better than nothin. Better than stayin home.

DWAYNE: Shel, aren't ya a little happy? I picked ya up in a cab.

SHELLY: Yeah. Y'know? I never been to the track before.

DWAYNE: I bet ya love it. Da usedta take me here when I was a kid. To see the horsies.

SHELLY: Horsies. Who'd ya get ta sit for us?

DWAYNE: Karen. She was the only one I could get.

SHELLY: That floozy. Did ya tell her she can't have no boyfriends over?

DWAYNE: Yeah. I told her no boyfriends. Come on, ya gotta stay in the line.

SHELLY: The only reason she sits for us cheap is so she can have a place ta get laid.

DWAYNE: *(laughs)* I know.

SHELLY: What a floozy ta have next door. She's lucky she's reliable.

DWAYNE: Hey. Can ya try an be in a stable mood? We're finally gettin out a night...

SHELLY: ...I'm tryin. So when are we goin ta the movie? If it's leavin?

DWAYNE: We'll go this weekend or somethin.

SHELLY: We can't afford ta go on the weekend. This is the last welfare Tuesday.

DWAYNE: Then we'll haveta get it when it comes out on video.

SHELLY: Sure. We'll get as far as the F.B.I. warnin an then the tape gets chewed.

DWAYNE: I'd say we're gonna get a new one very soon.

SHELLY: The vcr we got's so old. I'm suprised its not madea fuckin wood.

DWAYNE: Hey. I don't know if I should take ya in there. Ya might scare the horses.

[*HE kisses her.*]

SHELLY: I got the grossest proposition today. Those army guys are so dirty...

DWAYNE: I told ya. If that's happenin, then just fuckin quit the place.

SHELLY: Just cause I'm their waitress doesn't mean I got no dignity as a person.

DWAYNE: Why don't ya just pour boilin water on them or
somethin?.. Stay in line.

SHELLY: Ya want to hear what this guy said ta me?

DWAYNE: No, I don't wanna hear what he said ta ya. I
want ya ta quit.

SHELLY: Ya know I can't quit. How can I quit now?

DWAYNE: Well, there's gotta be somethin better than that
base.

[pause]

SHELLY: Did ya call down Manpower today?

DWAYNE: Yeah, I called. There wasn't anythin new.

SHELLY: Did ya call? Dwayne, ya have ta be aggressive.

DWAYNE: Shel. I'm bein aggressive. I called. There's nothin
for me.

SHELLY: Ya know ya have ta call in every day. Ya can't
miss a single day.

DWAYNE: There's no sense in callin every day. There's no
new projects.

SHELLY: But, there could be vacancies, or disability leaves...

DWAYNE: Hey, if I hear of a busload of machinists goin off
Kelly's mountain...

SHELLY: I'm just tryin ta help ya...

DWAYNE: I know you are but I just fuckin hate makin
those calls.

[pause]

SHELLY: I know ya do. I hate makin them too. Ya just have to.

DWAYNE: I'm gonna get somethin sooner or later.

SHELLY: We're gonna get outta the hole, sweetie.

DWAYNE: I know we are too. Ya gotta be a little patient.

SHELLY: I know. It's just my sickness talkin. That's all.

[SHE hugs him.]

DWAYNE: Could we maybe have a good time tonight?

63

SHELLY: Yeah. When ya go out ya gotta not think. Ya go out ta lose yourself.

DWAYNE: Ya don't have ta take that off here, there's a washroom in there, y'know.

SHELLY: I got the whole fuckin menu on my blouse an I gotta take it off, now.

DWAYNE: Do ya have to take it off with all these other people standin around?

SHELLY: You know I can't stand havin scummy clothes on. I hate bein greasy.

DWAYNE: C'mere. I like ya greasy. Gimme a little kiss.

SHELLY: Dwayne. You're gonna mess my lipstick an I don't got much left.

DWAYNE: Well, who're ya puttin the lipstick on for if it ain't for me? Huh?

SHELLY: Go for it, then.

DWAYNE: Can ya hurry it up? Those guys over there are starin at ya.

SHELLY: If ya don't like them starin at me, say somethin ta them about it.

DWAYNE: Shel. They're gonna look at ya if you're doin a fuckin striptease. I would.

SHELLY: I got big droopy tits. I'm a cow. They must get turned on by cattle.

DWAYNE: So, ya want me ta get into a fight over ya is that it? Ta prove myself?

SHELLY: *(teasing)* Na. We couldn't afford a funeral right now.

DWAYNE: It's gonna be your funeral ya keep pushin me...

SHELLY: Oh yeah? Someone's gotta keep ya in line, don't they?

[*THEY play-fight.*]

DWAYNE: Ya messed your lipstick for me?

SHELLY: Cause. I love ya. I don't want ya ta die, ever.

DWAYNE: How much do ya love me?

SHELLY: How much? Like, how many pounds?

DWAYNE: Yeah.

SHELLY: How bout... I love ya more than Disneyworld.

DWAYNE: How the hell do ya know that? You never been ta Disneyworld.

SHELLY: Yeah. But I know what Disneyworld looks like. Everybody does...

DWAYNE: So ya love me more than Disneyworld, do ya?

SHELLY: We have ta go ta Disneyworld. Can we go drive ta Disneyworld someday?

DWAYNE: Sure we can.

SHELLY: I keep meanin ta go ta the flea markets ta find a car seat.

DWAYNE: We won't haveta put our baby in someone else's car seat. We'll buy one.

SHELLY: Oh my God. Wouldn't Melissa just shit herself if she saw Disneyworld?

DWAYNE: She shits herself anway.

SHELLY: Yeah. She's so cute when she does it, though.

DWAYNE: ... Long as she doesn't shit on Mickey and get us kicked out.

[*SHELLY stops, suddenly.*]

SHELLY: Dwayne. There's a puddle. Who put that puddle there on the path?

DWAYNE: I don't know. It's just there. It musta rained last night.

SHELLY: I'm wearin my nice shoes. I didn't think there'd be mud at the movies.

[*DWAYNE hoists her up and over it.*]

SHELLY: Wheeee....oh, that was fun. Can ya do it again? Pick me up, please.

[*HE does.*]

DWAYNE: That's better than Disneyworld. An it didn't cost us nothin, did it?

SHELLY: If we could win some money at the track, can we get the car outta the shop?

DWAYNE: All ya gotta do is get the right horse once. An we got one tonight.

SHELLY: We do? Ya know who's gonna win? Ya really know who's gonna win?

[*HE shushes her.*]

DWAYNE: *(louder)* Yeah. It's a sin. Who's gonna... sin...Yeah...

SHELLY: Yeah. It's a sin. It's a total sin..Someone's goin ta hell for that one. That sin.

DWAYNE: Yeah. What a sin. *(to the ticket taker)* Two please.

SHELLY: Hey. Ya really know who's gonna win the races?

DWAYNE: Onea them. Shh.

[*pause*]

SHELLY: They say it only takes three days drivin ta Florida.

DWAYNE: Three days...

SHELLY: Yeah. It ain't that far at all, really. As the crow flies.

[*THEY pass through the gate. The sounds of the track become very loud.*]

SCENE 2

A bench. SHELLY and DWAYNE arriving. DWAYNE sits and studies a racing form, SHELLY eats popcorn.

SHELLY: So where's all the horses at? All I see around here are pigeons.

DWAYNE: They got em in the stables gettin ready. They bring em out for the races.

SHELLY: So how do ya know who's gonna win? Did ya get a hot tip or somethin?

DWAYNE: I don't wanna talk about this where someone could overhear it.

SHELLY: There's no one near us. Those guys over there don't know us.

DWAYNE: I'm a little superstitious. I don't like talkin too much...

SHELLY: Do I have ta give ya the tickle torture?

DWAYNE: No, ya don't have ta do that. Ya definitely don't. Shel...please...

[SHE tickles him.]

SHELLY: I know everywhere you're ticklish. We got no secrets....

DWAYNE: *(calling over)* Hey, Wally...How's it goin?

SHELLY: Who's that skid? Wally. Ya know him?

DWAYNE: Yeah. I don't know him too well. I ain't seen him in ages.

SHELLY: How do ya know him? Did he go ta school with us?

DWAYNE: I don't know. I maybe met him out vocational or somethin.

SHELLY: Well, why ya hidin from him? He was gonna come over an say 'hi'.

DWAYNE: I ain't hidin. I just don't want him ta come ask me if I'm workin now.

SHELLY: Okay then. Tell me about the baby. Did she say any new words today?

DWAYNE: I don't know. She said the usual words. No new ones.

[*pause*]

SHELLY: Maybe she's only gonna have a three word vocabulary. What if that's it?

DWAYNE: She's fine. Don't go gettin paranoid now.

SHELLY: 'Mama', 'Dadda', an 'No'. How far's she gonna get in life with three words?

DWAYNE: There's nothin wrong with our baby's head. It's your head.

SHELLY: It ain't my head. It's that gas or propane or whatever's leakin in our place.

DWAYNE: It's probly just a dead skunk or somethin. That smell's probly harmless.

SHELLY: Yeah. Probly. Oh, that's a nice neighbor ta have.

DWAYNE: We're gonna move above ground soon as things start lookin up.

SHELLY: We won't have ta buy a pet for Melissa when she gets older...

DWAYNE: There's nothin wrong with the baby...

SHELLY: She can play with the decomposin skunk in the laundry room.

[*Pause.*] [*SHE touches him.*]

DWAYNE: Why do ya want to make things hurt more?

SHELLY: Remember when...we usedta have pet names for each other? Remember?

DWAYNE: Yeah. When we were goin out.

SHELLY: Can we have pet names again? Gimme a pet name.

DWAYNE: What. Right now?

SHELLY: Yeah. Gimme a pet name again. Like we're in love for the first time.

DWAYNE: I don't know. I'd have ta think about that a bit.

SHELLY: No. Just gimme one for right now. But gimme somethin I'll like, okay?

DWAYNE: *(pause)* Winnebago.

SHELLY: Winnebago? That's what ya want ta call me for a pet name.

DWAYNE: *(laughs)* Ya said give ya somethin y'll like. Ya like Winnebagos.

SHELLY: Why do ya want ta call me that? Cause I'm big an roomy, I suppose.

DWAYNE: I love ya the way ya are. You're the love of my life forever.

[pause]

SHELLY: Why do ya go out all the time at nights if I'm the lovea your life?

DWAYNE: I'm workin at the club those nights. That's the only nights I'm goin out.

SHELLY: You're not comin down the track those nights?

DWAYNE: Na. This is a special occasion. I ain't been down here in years.

SHELLY: So, is Leo ever gonna pay ya for those shifts ya worked bar for him?

DWAYNE: Yeah. When he gets the money, we're gonna get the money.

[pause]

SHELLY: You're not over Leo's bar boffin some chick that's skinnier than me?

DWAYNE: I'm not goin with any other women.

SHELLY: I'm only eatin causea anxiety. I think I still got some post partum depression.

DWAYNE: I know. Ya had a hard time, with havin the baby.

[SHE snatches the racing form.]

SHELLY: If our race isn't runnin till later, why are ya readin the papers now?

DWAYNE: I was just lookin at it for fun. Tryin ta pick the winners.

SHELLY: This race here is comin up next? Ya circled "Glory Days".

DWAYNE: Yeah? So?

SHELLY: Why didn't ya pick "Heartspent"?

DWAYNE: Cause it's a long shot. It's long odds. He's probly gonna lose.

[*SHE gives it back.*]

SHELLY: Heartspent is a "she".

DWAYNE: *(laughs)* Oh, she is, is she? How the hell do you know?

SHELLY: I bet she is. I want ta put a bet down on Heartspent. How do ya go do it?

DWAYNE: What are ya talkin about? Ya want to bet?

SHELLY: I wanna make a bet for myself. Ya think only the guy makes the gambles?

DWAYNE: I'll put the bet down for ya. But I'll tell ya, that horse ain't gonna win.

SHELLY: How are ya surea that? You don't know much about horse racin either..

DWAYNE: Cause. I can tell. I know more than you...

SHELLY: I like her cause she got a heart in her name. An I got my money from tips.

DWAYNE: Heartspent. When the heart gets spent, ya die. You're bettin on a dead horse.

SHELLY: *(laughs)* It's my horse. Don't go kickin my dead horse.

DWAYNE: I'm just sayin, ya shouldn't go wastein your tip money on a gluebag.

SHELLY: I'm havin fun. And stop insultin my friggin horse. Here's five bucks.

DWAYNE: Would ya bet on him if he was named Dogfood?

SHELLY: I'm not listenin. Go make the bet for me.

DWAYNE: Eight sixteen ta one. He's probly sponsored by Doctor Ballard's puppy chow.

SHELLY: While you're goin ta bet, I'm gonna call Karen, check on the baby.

DWAYNE: Bet ya anythin she's on the phone when ya try ta call.

SHELLY: Yeah. Givin her boyfriends phone sex. She better be feedin Melly.

DWAYNE: There's a pay phone in the grandstand, I think.

SHELLY: Hey, sweetie, you were right. This is kinda fun...

[*HE watches her wander away. HE looks at the money in his hand and goes off to bet.*]

SCENE 3

DWAYNE, sitting alone with his racing form. After a moment, SHELLY enters, eating fries.

DWAYNE: I made the bet. Your race is comin up in a few minutes.

SHELLY: Oh. Ya want some fries? They're really good fries here.

DWAYNE: Thanks, baby. I'm not too hungry right now.

SHELLY: Dwayne. You been losin weight. Ya have ta eat sometimes.

DWAYNE: Did ya get a holda the babysitter? How's Melly doin? Is she sleepin?

SHELLY: It was still busy. You were right. Ya tell her no boyfriends...

DWAYNE: She ends up talkin ta them all night on the phone.

SHELLY: I'll haveta soak the phone receiver in Javex when I get home.

[The starter's horn blows. A short blast.]

DWAYNE: Why eatin your fries like that? Ya think you're
    Princess Di?

SHELLY: It's not high falutin. I just got a little class, that's
    all.

DWAYNE: Oh. class, eh? I didn't know I was married into
    the Royal Family.

SHELLY: Shut up. I just want a new vcr so I can do my
    workout videos again.

DWAYNE: We'll have ta get a bigger place just so you can
    do your jumpin jacks.

[pause]

SHELLY: Dwayne. Do I still turn ya on, though? Are ya still
    in love with me?

DWAYNE: I bet ya don't even realize how much I'm in love
    with ya.

SHELLY: I'm gonna go on this diet soon, ya only eat crackers,
    water, and oranges.

DWAYNE: I don't want ya ta go on a diet. You're too pretty
    for me as it is.

[SHE cuddles him.]

SHELLY: Sweetie, ya got dirt on your face. Didn't ya wash
    yourself today?

DWAYNE: What are ya? Mama Raccoon? Ya don't have ta
    wash me...

SHELLY: Just cause we're broke we don't gotta look like
    the resta these skids here.

DWAYNE: Well, we ain't gonna be broke forever. I know
    that for sure.

SHELLY: We just gotta get outta the hole. The whole world'll
    look different.

DWAYNE: An the backhoe's gonna stop dumpin loads on us.

[The starter's horn blows. Longer blast.]

SHELLY: Did I tell ya the collection agent from Sears called me at work today?

DWAYNE: No, they didn't. Did they?

SHELLY: Yeah. It's a good thing I answered. I woulda been fuckin mortified.

DWAYNE: How'd they get your work number?

SHELLY: I don't know. Collection agencies know everythin. They got computers.

DWAYNE: Ya know what I was thinkin we could do. Ta get them off our backs?

SHELLY: What?

DWAYNE: We could call Cape Breton Post an get them ta print our obituaries.

SHELLY: I wanna make a little payment, so can I take it from your next cheque?

DWAYNE: Yeah. Not this cheque comin up?

SHELLY: Of course, this one. This is your last one. Ya got no more stamps.

[pause]

DWAYNE: Did ya tell them you're tryin? They can wait if ya tell them.

SHELLY: Dwayne, I was embarrassed. They only want a little $30 dollar payment.

DWAYNE: We already owe this cheque.

SHELLY: Ya already owe it? Ya don't even got it yet. Who do ya owe it to?

DWAYNE: You know what bills we got same as I do. I got it worked out home.

SHELLY: I wasn't countin on your last cheque bein used up before we got it.

DWAYNE: I'll get the money from Leo this week an you can make your payment.

SHELLY: You're gonna get the money from Leo? We could
        use it, next week is rent.
DWAYNE: I'll get the money from Leo.
SHELLY: Ya better get the money from Leo, or I'm gonna
        go talk ta Leo.
DWAYNE: No, you're not.
SHELLY: Arsehole. He's just takin advantage of ya cause
        ya got a good nature.
DWAYNE: Just let me handle some things my own way.
        Alright?

[*pause*]

SHELLY: Dwayne. Maybe you could join the army.
DWAYNE: Huh? Ya want me ta be like those pigs ya haveta
        serve all day?
SHELLY: The army might be pigs but at least they got a
        lotta money in their pockets.
DWAYNE: Yeah. Ya like their pockets, don't ya? I bet ya
        love what's in their pockets.

[*pause*]

SHELLY: Are ya talkin filthy? Is that what that's supposed
        ta mean?
DWAYNE: Can ya trust me? Do ya think ya can trust me
        when I do things?
SHELLY: Then do somethin. Anythin. Just, be your old self
        again.
DWAYNE: I'm gonna find somethin sooner or later.

[*The sound of horses. Drawing nearer.*]

SHELLY: Dwayne? Did ya ever thinka goin to collection
        agencies?
DWAYNE: Why would I go ta them?

SHELLY: Did ya see there's this ad in the paper all week hirin collection agents?

[*pause*]

DWAYNE: Are ya serious? Tell me you're not serious...

SHELLY: I know its bad. But ya don't have ta have experience...it says...

DWAYNE: I got a little fuckin self-respect, okay? There's things ya don't stoop to.

SHELLY: I wouldn't like it either. But maybe ya have ta go with the times.

DWAYNE: Ya want me ta be a professional prick? Is that your dream for me?

SHELLY: If we both had steady money comin in, we could start makin our dreams.

DWAYNE: I'd sooner shovel shit. I'd rather work for no pay at fuckin Burger King.

SHELLY: Well, it looks like beggars can't be choosers, right?

DWAYNE: I ain't stupid, ya know. I got fuckin trainin. Ta do somethin with my life.

SHELLY: I know ya do. I'm just thinkin about your happiness...

DWAYNE: Happiness. Ya gotta have some dignity, okay? Or you're just an animal.

SHELLY: Dwayne?

[*pause*]

DWAYNE: What? Ya got any more genius ideas?

SHELLY: Yeah. I love you.

[*SHE holds him.*]

DWAYNE: Do ya?

SHELLY: Of course I do. Always. I got faith in ya.

DWAYNE: Ya do? Ya really do?

[*HER attention is drawn to the track, as the horses approach.*]

SHELLEY: Hey. Look at the horses! Wow. There they are..
DWAYNE: Come on closer. Have a look.
SHELLY: Dwayne? They'd never jump over the railing would they? An stomp us?
DWAYNE: How they gonna jump over the rail? They're all harnessed up.
SHELLY: My horsey. They're so beautiful. Where's mine? Where's Heartspent?
DWAYNE: He's number 12. Number 12 is Heartspent.
SHELLY: C'mon Heartspent! Oh, isn't she gorgeous? She looks so tired though.
DWAYNE: Na. These are all just two year olds. They're still babies.

[*THEY watch them trot past.*]

SHELLY: They're so proud lookin. An strong. Are they tame or wild?
DWAYNE: I'd say they're pretty wild. I wouldn't wanna be their dentist.
SHELLY: *(sings)* "...Wild, wild horses...couldn't drag me...away..."
DWAYNE: The Stones...
SHELLY: Remember I usedta play that tape all the time in our first little apartment?
DWAYNE: Yeah. That was a great old song.
SHELLY: *(laughs)* Yeah, it was. Till it got eaten.

[*There is the starter's call. The race begins in the dark.*]

SCENE 4

The race is in progress, near the end. DWAYNE and SHELLY are standing on the bench, screaming, urging them on.

DWAYNE: ...Straightaway! Homestretch!

SHELLY: Go Heartspent! Don't get tired...

DWAYNE: Straightaway! Bring it home...

SHELLY: Run! Heartspent!

DWAYNE: Stretch Baby...You're on the stretch...Come on home!

SHELLY: You're wild baby! Come on...

[*The horses closer. Very loud.*]

DWAYNE: She's explodin! Look at her...

SHELLY: GO!...GO...

DWAYNE: Straight home!

SHELLY: Don't let em catch up!

DWAYNE: *(ecstatic)* Straight fuckin home!...

[*The horses pass them. Deafening.*]

SHELLY: GO!...Finish...

DWAYNE: All the way, straight fuckin home!

SHELLY: Home!...Heartspent? Heartspent?

[*pause*]

DWAYNE: I can't believe it.

SHELLY: What? Did she come first? It looked like she was first from here. Didn't it?

DWAYNE: Holy Jesus, get your cross! Ya won! Ya won ya dummy! Ya flukie, baby!

SHELLY: I won? Heartspent won?

77

DWAYNE: Look at it up there on the toteboard! It's gonna
    come up on the big board!

[SHE freaks out.]

SHELLY: We won! We won! I told ya. I told ya. Didn't I tell
    ya?
DWAYNE: Yeah. Ya told me...
SHELLY: I told ya, didn't I? Don't say I didn't tell ya cause
    I told ya she was gonna win!
DWAYNE: Ya did. I don't know how the hell ya did...
SHELLY: Well don't ask me cause I couldn't tell ya! Oh,
    god. I think I peed my pants.
DWAYNE: See, I told ya it was a special time out for us an
    it's gonna get even better.
SHELLY: Dwayne. Maybe I can do it everytime! Maybe
    I'm a psychic friend.
DWAYNE: I don't know. Maybe ya can. How did ya do it?
SHELLY: I just kinda read down the lista the horses. An I
    got a special kinda feelin.
DWAYNE: How? What kinda feelin? What did the feelin
    feel like?
SHELLY: I don't know. A...special feelin, that's all. Kinda
    like...when I seen you.
DWAYNE: When ya seen me? What do ya mean?
SHELLY: Y'know. The first time I seen ya. I knew I was
    gonna marry ya. I knew.
DWAYNE: Yeah? Ya did? You never ever told me that be-
    fore.

[SHE kisses him.]

SHELLY: I won, didn't I?
DWAYNE: Ya sure did. We both won. An no one can take it
    away.
SHELLY: That's right. They can't! We won, and it's all ours...
DWAYNE: ...Just wait till our next race.

SHELLY: I won! I won! I won! I won! I won!
DWAYNE: *(laughs)* Ya don't gotta rub it in on people.
SHELLY: But...I really won somethin. It wasn't someone else...

[*pause*]

DWAYNE: Hey. I don't want ta rain on ya but ya only won
about $40 bucks.
SHELLY: Oh. That's all? Oh. Cause I only made a little
bet. Shit...

[*pause*]

DWAYNE: Hey. It's still $40 bucks. It's forty bucks ya made
outta $5 bucks.
SHELLY: I shoulda bet more. I shoulda bet more. Why didn't
I trust myself?
DWAYNE: Ya want put money down on my bet, ya can do
it. I'm goin ta put it in now.
SHELLY: Yeah?
DWAYNE: Ya got money from tips. How much money did
ya make on your tips today?
SHELLY: Thirty somethin dollars. Maybe $40...
DWAYNE: Black Silence is over six ta one. That could be
$200 more bucks.
SHELLY: Black Silence. Is that the horse ya got the tip on?
Black Silence?
DWAYNE: Yeah. I got it from a guy. This guy, he works at
the stables over there.
SHELLY: Oh. How did ya get the tip from him?
DWAYNE: I don't know. I just know him. I seen him on the
street an he told me.
SHELLY: Ya seen him on the street? On our street?
DWAYNE: There's a damn good reason why that horse is
gonna win.
SHELLY: So what's the reason then?
DWAYNE: There's a very very very good reason.

[*pause*]

SHELLY: I guess ya gotta go big or go home. That's what I
shoulda done last time.
DWAYNE: I got inside information on this. Ya must have a
good feelin about it.
SHELLY: Who's puttin who on? I ain't psychic. I got lucky
the last time.
DWAYNE: So. Are ya gonna go for it with me?
SHELLY: Where'd you get money ta bet, anyways? From
what I gave ya last night?
DWAYNE: Yeah. An I scrounged around the house. Are ya
gonna go for it?

[*pause*]

SHELLY: I can see how some people get addicted ta this.
It's too damn fun.
DWAYNE: No. You stay here. I'll go make the bet. I can do it...
SHELLY: Why do ya always wanna go in alone? I want ta
go claim my winnings.
DWAYNE: Shel. I'm gonna be in line. Ya know how ya
hate standin in line.
SHELLY: Yeah, but I hate waitin around alone on benches
just as much.
DWAYNE: I got your stub in my pocket. Ya wanna put your
winnings on it, too?

[*pause*]

SHELLY: Sure. What the hell. If Black Silence comes in,
we'll have a movie fest.
DWAYNE: You bet we will. You deserve it for workin so
hard.

[HE kisses her, exits.]

SHELLY: We could get a new vcr with a remote for only $300 bucks.

DWAYNE: Yeah? Then we're gettin one.

SHELLY: Hey. If ya got a quarter, see if ya can get through ta Karen the Call Girl.

DWAYNE: Okay. I'll try.

[*DWAYNE is gone. SHELLY takes out the remains of her popcorn bag and eats.*]

SHELLY: Ya gotta take a leap of faith every now an then. *(SHE throws a piece.)* You pigeons are lucky cause ya got wings for that. *(pause)* If you pigeons got such beautiful wings, why do ya spend all your time down here in the muck an shit?

[*SHE pulls her jacket around her. It is colder, becoming night.*]

SCENE 5

About 15 minutes later. SHELLY is huddled up on the bench. DWAYNE enters, putting the new stub in his pocket.

SHELLY: Who was that guy you were talkin to over by the bettin booth?

DWAYNE: Ya seen me in there? He was just some fella I met while I was in line.

SHELLY: When ya were havin such a chummy time, did ya thinka me out here?

[*pause*]

DWAYNE: Shel. How can ya have a mood swing after we just won like that?

SHELLY: I just wanna know. How come the pigeons won't eat my popcorn?

DWAYNE: What are ya talkin about?

SHELLY: I been tryin ta feed them popcorn an they all keep flyin away.

DWAYNE: It's nothin personal. It's nightime. They're all gone back ta their nests.

SHELLY: Friggin little moochers. The government should just kill them all.

DWAYNE: *(laughs)* An I thought ya loved animals.

SHELLY: What are you? The fuckin SPCA? You wouldn't let Melissa have a puppy.

DWAYNE: Yeah. She's only nine months old. We talked about this before.

SHELLY: Her and the puppy could grow up together. Puppies aren't expensive...

[*pause*]

DWAYNE: You gotta take those pills for your hormones, Shel. I can't take this.

SHELLY: You never mind my fuckin hormones! They're my hormones, not yours!

DWAYNE: Well, I ain't your yo-yo ta play with, y'know?

SHELLY: Well, I got this hormone imbalance havin your baby. Did ya call Karen?

DWAYNE: Yeah, I called Karen.

SHELLY: So did ya get through or is it still busy?

DWAYNE: No. It's still busy. Forget it. Can ya just try ta have fun, okay?

SHELLY: I can't have any fun thinkin about our baby in that apartment...

DWAYNE: There's no poison in our apartment. I'm positive.

SHELLY: There's gas leak somewhere. You know there's somethin. You smell it too.

DWAYNE: If there's a bad smell sometimes, so what? It's harmless.

SHELLY: If it's harmless, what happened ta all the mice then? Where did they go?

DWAYNE: Someone upstairs musta bought a cat. Listen ta yourself. Ya sound crazy.

SHELLY: It's not crazy. I got a lotta concerns about this situation...

DWAYNE: I got them too, Shel. How many times are we gonna go through it?

SHELLY: When you start doin somethin about it! I'm tryin ta support this family!

[*pause*]

DWAYNE: I am doin somethin about it. I bought the traps. I put out traps.

SHELLY: They were always empty. Where did the mice go? They left causea the gas!

DWAYNE: No, they didn't. There's no gas. There's no fuckin gas leak.

SHELLY: Why do we haveta live in a fuckin basement? Why can't we be upstairs?

DWAYNE: Someone upstairs got a cat...the cat chased them out.

SHELLY: I never seen a cat around our place. If there's a cat, then show me a cat.

[*DWAYNE loses it.*]

DWAYNE: Ya want me ta show ya a cat, Shel? We get home, I'll show ya a fuckin cat!

SHELLY: Sure ya will. How ya gonna show me a cat if it doesn't even exist?

DWAYNE: I'll find the cat that's eatin our mice an I'll kill the fuckin thing!

SHELLY: Yeah. So now you're gonna make a scene? That's helpful...

DWAYNE: Ya want the mice back? Ya want ta see no gas? I'll kill the fuckin cat!

SHELLY: No, ya won't. I bet you couldn't find it, let alone kill it!

DWAYNE: I'll find it, an kill it, and I'll nail it to a stick. Stick it in the yard for ya!

SHELLY: That's disgusting!

DWAYNE: Then you'll have your mice everywhere. Crawlin up your legs, inta your...

SHELLY: Shut up! Is that how much ya love me?

DWAYNE: Yeah. Will that be doin somethin enough for ya?

[*pause*]

SHELLY: Dwayne? Is this how much ya love me?

DWAYNE: Will that be enough for ya? Will that show ya that I'm fuckin tryin?

SHELLY: Stop, or I'm gonna leave...

DWAYNE: You're gonna leave? Do ya know how close I get ta leavin?

[*The starter's horn blows. A short blast.*]

SHELLY: Dwayne. Can't ya see how sick I am?

DWAYNE: I know you're sick. But you're makin me sick too...

SHELLY: I know you never took a sick day in your life...

DWAYNE: Why do ya have ta try and break me down all the time?

SHELLY: I know I'm psycho. But when ya love someone there's gotta be no limits.

DWAYNE: There's no limits.

SHELLY: Ma says that all the time. She heard it from Billy Graham or someone.

DWAYNE: Everyone's got their breakin point.

SHELLY: Do ya feel like sometimes we're turnin inta monsters?

84

[pause]

DWAYNE: I don't know. I think you are, sometimes.

SHELLY: I just want a little light in the windows. That's all I want. That ain't much.

DWAYNE: After this horse comes in for us, we're gonna move upstairs.

SHELLY: If ya have some dreams, then ya never get so low ya can't get up.

DWAYNE: Well, we always get up, don't we? An we're gonna get upstairs.

SHELLY: Could we maybe move inta my Ma's house? Till we get another place.

DWAYNE: Who? Who's movin inta your Ma's house?

SHELLY: Who else? Me an the baby an you.

DWAYNE: Me move inta your house again. That'd go over like a fart in church.

SHELLY: She doesn't got much, but it's ours if we want.

DWAYNE: Yeah, an we're right back where we started three years ago.

SHELLY: We wouldn't have ta tell your father...

DWAYNE: He always knows when we're in trouble. He's got a sixth fuckin sense.

SHELLY: What's more important, Dwayne? Your sensea pride or our baby's health?

DWAYNE: Ya can't run away all the time, Shel. Ya can't go runnin home ta Mama.

SHELLY: I just want ta get her away from that smell. Whatever it is. I'm scared.

DWAYNE: If we move ta your house, they'll laugh an say "See..ya weren't ready.."

SHELLY: I don't care. It's nonea their damn business! It's just a little while. Please?

DWAYNE: We wouldn't be able ta sleep together if we went ta your house.

SHELLY: Yes, we would. Cause we're married now.

DWAYNE: You know what I mean. Your Mother Theresa couldn't handle us doin it.

SHELLY: If that's what ya mean, then we barely do it anymore now anyway.

[*pause*]

DWAYNE: Shel. We do so. We do it all the time...

SHELLY: I know it's cause I'm a fat cow. An I got my mood swings.

DWAYNE: Maybe we ain't done it a lot lately, but it doesn't mean nothin.

SHELLY: Ya go through so much shit together. It's hard ta remember love.

[*The starters horn blows. A longer blast.*]

DWAYNE: The race is gonna start soon. That horn means it's post time.

[*pause*]

SHELLY: So are ya ever gonna tell me what the big tip is?

DWAYNE: About Black Silence?

SHELLY: Yeah. Why is he gonna win? Why are ya so sure we got a winner?

DWAYNE: They say ya can't win big here without inside information.

SHELLY: So what's the information? I put money on it. You better tell me.

[*pause*]

DWAYNE: What I got is...I found out Black Silence is gettin his first shots today.

SHELLY: Gettin his first shots for what?

DWAYNE: For rabies, Shel. What do ya think? Somethin ta make him go faster.

SHELLY: Ya mean he's gettin drugged? Is that why he's gonna win?

DWAYNE: Yeah. But they're all drugged up. Just...Black Silence is gettin his first dose.

SHELLY: All the horses are drugged. How do ya know all this? From the stable guy?

DWAYNE: Cause the other ones got...a tolerance now. Black Silence got no tolerance.

SHELLY: What do they shoot them with? What's in the needles?

DWAYNE: Adrenalin or somethin. Steroids. Who cares? It makes em faster. That's it.

[*pause*]

SHELLY: That's sick! Ya mean all those beautiful horses are...like junkies?

DWAYNE: Shel. C'mon. Ya musta known that. Everyone knows that.

[*The sound of horses, drawing nearer.*]

SHELLY: Black Silence. Why don't they just call him after fuckin Ben Johnson?

DWAYNE: I don't care if he's named after Johnson an Johnson's Baby Powder...

SHELLY: That's corrupted!

DWAYNE: As long as he wins the race. I got this for us. Can ya be a little grateful?

SHELLY: So that's the way it is, I guess. Where is he? Is he onea those over there?

DWAYNE: In just a few minutes, we're gonna have a lotta money from this.

SHELLY: It says he's number eight. There's no number eight out there.

DWAYNE: Of course there is. There's gotta be a number eight.

SHELLY: They're goin right past us an I don't see any number eights.

[*HE takes the racing form.*]

DWAYNE: Ya musta looked at the number wrong. This is his race. I put the bet down.

SHELLY: There he is.

DWAYNE: Black Silence? Where?

SHELLY: Over there. Bringin up the rear.

[*THEY stare at the horse.*]

DWAYNE: It can't be.

SHELLY: How old is he supposedta be? He ain't two years old. Are there horse years?

[*pause*]

DWAYNE: Fuck..fuck..fuck..oh my fuck..

SHELLY: It looks like they had ta give him drugs just ta make him stand up.

DWAYNE: He has ta drop out. He has ta drop out. He can't run a race like that...

SHELLY: His head keeps jerkin up over his shoulder. Why's he..?

DWAYNE: Oh God...

SHELLY: The poor baby. He looks like he's sufferin.

DWAYNE: We gotta get our money back. We gotta...He has ta drop out...

[*DWAYNE runs.*]

SHELLY: Can they make him drop out? Can they?..

DWAYNE: *(screams)* He has ta drop out!

[The starters call.]

*[The race is run in the dark. As the race goes on,
DWAYNE'S voice can be heard in the darkness,
laughing. It is hysterical laughter. It goes on and
on, floating in the night above the thunder of the
horses. The race ends.]*

SCENE 6

The bench. Later. DWAYNE sits, vacant, holding the
racing stub in his fist. SHELLY sits on the opposite side
of the bench from him.

SHELLY: Dwayne? It's not that funny anymore. It was never
    funny.
DWAYNE: I know. It's not very funny at all, is it.

[pause]

SHELLY: They didn't give that poor horse adrenalin. It was
    more like heroin.
DWAYNE: He screwed it up somehow. He musta got over-
    dosed or somethin.
SHELLY: Over dosed. They overdosed the poor thing. Can
    we get outta here now? I'm overdosed, too.

[pause]

DWAYNE: I can't go home. I gotta do somethin about this.
SHELLY: Dwayne. The race ended over an hour ago. How
    long do ya wanna sit an stew?
DWAYNE: I have ta get our money back somehow.

SHELLY: Ya can't get it back. It's closed. They aren't gonna just give it back anyway.

DWAYNE: How much do ya love me now?

[*pause*]

SHELLY: We won some, an we lost some. I guess we ain't the first.

DWAYNE: We won some, didn't we? We won some.

SHELLY: Can we go home an stew about it? They're gonna lock the gates on us.

DWAYNE: They never lock the gates. Ya can stay all night if ya want.

SHELLY: That's great. But I don't wanna stay all night. I hope ya saved us cab money.

DWAYNE: *(more to himself)* What's the worst thing a person could do?

SHELLY: Come on. Get up. Quit actin like a Martian. Let's go home.

DWAYNE: I'm not goin.

[*pause*]

SHELLY: Ya got no money for a cab. Do ya? Is that what you're tellin me?

DWAYNE: I'm gonna get our money back.

SHELLY: Why didn't ya say so before gettin me ta bet all the cash I had on me?

DWAYNE: If you're gonna be like this, why don't ya just get home then!

[*pause*]

SHELLY: How? What am I supposedta do? Walk? There's no buses. How?

DWAYNE: I'm gonna go find that guy who gave me that tip. Over by the stables.

SHELLY: Why the hell do you gotta meet him at this hour?
  I haveta work tomorrow!
DWAYNE: I'm gonna take care of things for us. I'm gonna
  fix things, Shel.
SHELLY: Fix what? Ya can't get our money back. What are
  ya gonna fix? Tonight?
DWAYNE: I'm gonna fix everythin. I can do it.

[*pause*]

SHELLY: Baby. Let's just call a cab. We'll get him ta stop
  at the bank machine.
DWAYNE: It was gonna be so perfect. Straight fuckin home.
SHELLY: We'll get him ta stop at the machine up at Bar-
  gain Harold's. Y'know? An...
DWAYNE: He ran so hard for us. Did ya see the blood? All
  the blood...
SHELLY: ...Th-there's gonna be...money in our account, isn't
  there, Dwayne.
DWAYNE: ...There was blood pourin out of his nose. But he
  never quit.
SHELLY: Our rent money. For next month. It's there, isn't
  it? An the sitter...
DWAYNE: ...He just never had a chance, though. Never had
  a chance.

[*pause*]

SHELLY: How much did ya bet, Dwayne? How much did
  ya scrounge from the house?
DWAYNE: They killed him. Before he even got started.
SHELLY: How much did ya bet for us? On Black Silence.
  Show me the ticket.

[*HE starts to rip it up.*]

DWAYNE: Black Silence...was supposedta win.

91

SHELLY: Dwayne! Gimme the ticket! Gimme the stub or whatever it is!

DWAYNE: I'm gonna get it all back. I swear on my life.

[*SHE takes it from him.*]

SHELLY: F-five..hundred..ninety..

[*pause*]

DWAYNE: I'm gonna get that money back.

SHELLY: We got nothin in our account? Ya cleaned it out...on this night?

DWAYNE: I'm gonna take care of it. I promise.

SHELLY: That's everythin we have. Dwayne? Ya went into our account for...

DWAYNE: Why don't ya just go home now?

SHELLY: What home? We ain't gonna have enough money for rent! Now...

DWAYNE: I'm gonna pay it back. I swear. I'll pay it back with interest. I can...

SHELLY: How do ya think you're gonna pay this back? It wasn't yours ta *play* with...

DWAYNE: I'm gonna get it from the guy. Who gave us the tip. He owes us...

SHELLY: Oh, you're fuckin funny aren't ya? You can be the one ta go inta the Welfare!

DWAYNE: I'm gonna fix it, okay? Did ya hear me when I said I'll fix it?

SHELLY: You bastard! That's...that was my money! I made it. Not you! Are ya insane?

DWAYNE: I'm gonna fix it! I'm gonna fix it! I'm gonna fuckin *fix* it!

[*DWAYNE kicks the garbage can, hard, in a fury.*]

SHELLY: How could ya do this to us? How could ya?

[*pause*]

DWAYNE: It wasn't supposed ta happen...the way it happened. Y'know?

SHELLY: Why did ya take me here? Why did ya take me
here? I don't want ta be here.

DWAYNE: I thought ya might...want ta see the horses.

SHELLY: I wanted ta go see a movie. Dwayne? *How could ya*?

DWAYNE: Cause...ya love animals. I know how much ya
love animals.

SHELLY: I never wanted ta see these animals! I didn't need
ta ever see these animals!

[*SHE starts to cry.*]

DWAYNE: I'm gonna have a smoke right now. An then I'm
goin across...

SHELLY: Ya quit smokin, ya idiot. Don't ya remember?
Don't ya remember?

DWAYNE: I'm gonna go over the stables. An I'm gonna
find him. An then...

SHELLY: Look at ya. Smokin a fuckin ciggy butt off the
ground. How's the taste?

DWAYNE: ...Cause he guaranteed us. He guaranteed me I
had a winner!

SHELLY: He guaranteed ya, did he? That's great...

DWAYNE: He's gonna be out drinkin. They always go
drinkin after the races.

SHELLY: What are ya talkin about? Why can't ya fuckin
talk sensible?

DWAYNE: He's gonna haveta pay us back.

[*pause*]

SHELLY: How'd ya know they went drinkin after? Dwayne?
How did ya know?

DWAYNE: I don't know. They probly go drinkin.

SHELLY: No one just knows somethin. Ya....ya knew. Ya
knew they go out...cause...
DWAYNE: What?

[*pause*]

SHELLY: Ya come here every night. Don't ya.? Ya been
comin here all those nights.
DWAYNE: What nights? What are ya talkin about?

[*pause*]

SHELLY: That's why ya knew those people here. Ya said
they were your old friends.
DWAYNE: What people?
SHELLY: Ya said ya never seen them in ages! Ya probly see
them every night.
DWAYNE: I don't come here every night. I told ya. This
was...a special occasion.
SHELLY: An ya knew everywhere ta go. Ya knew perfectly
how ta do things.
DWAYNE: I usedta come here with Da, alright. He showed
me how...
SHELLY: Ya even knew where the bathrooms were right
off the bat!
DWAYNE: It ain't hard ta forget where the bathrooms are
in a place! Is it?
SHELLY: Ya got addicted. Didn't ya?

[*pause*]

DWAYNE: I'm not addicted. This was a special occasion. It
was gonna be...
SHELLY: Oh, it's fuckin special alright, Dwayne! I'll never
forget this occasion.
DWAYNE: Now, don't go bein paranoid.

94

SHELLY: That's how ya knew. They were open all night. They never closed..

DWAYNE: *(angry)* I told ya. I usedta come here with my Da. That's why...

SHELLY: I was sittin home worryin you were out fuckin some bimbo at the bar...

DWAYNE: You're so paranoid. Listen to ya. This is morea that poison gas, isn't it?

SHELLY: But you were here. At the track. Fuckin yourself instead.

DWAYNE: That's it. I'm leavin. You just go fuck *your* self...

SHELLY: Weren't ya? Fuckin everything...we worked for. Oh my God...

DWAYNE: Ya think I been comin here all those nights? Is that what ya think?

SHELLY: I bet ya got the money from Leo for the car. An ya blew it, didn't ya?

DWAYNE: I never got any money for the car. Are ya callin me a liar now?

SHELLY: An your last cheque already gone. Dwayne? Do ya even got a job at Leo's?

DWAYNE: What are you talkin about? Do I got a job at Leo's. What?

SHELLY: Did ya *ever*? That's why ya wouldn't let me call. Or drop by to see ya...

DWAYNE: Now you're callin me a liar! Ya never trust me this fuckin much!

SHELLY: Don't hit me. Don't you dare hit me!

DWAYNE: Hit ya? I never hit ya once in my whole life! Am I a wife beater too now?

[*pause*]

SHELLY: I don't know. I don't know what ya are now.

DWAYNE: Ya think I'm addicted? Ya think I got no control over my comin here?

SHELLY: I don't know. Let's just get outta here, okay? I hate this place.

[*pause*]

DWAYNE: No way. I ain't goin back home empty handed.
SHELLY: Ya think that guy's gonna just hand ya over $600 bucks?
DWAYNE: Yeah. Why shouldn't he? It's all his fault we lost everything.
SHELLY: He works in a fuckin stable! What's he gonna pay ya with. Straw?
DWAYNE: It isn't my fault. He's the one. He made us lose.
SHELLY: Dwayne? What do ya think you're gonna do? There's nothin ya can do.
DWAYNE: Nothin? I can rip his fuckin head off an shit down his neck for a start.
SHELLY: Ya didn't haveta take his advice. An you ain't a fighter, Dwayne...

[*DWAYNE suddenly grabs her by the throat.*]

DWAYNE: I ain't a fighter? Ya think I'm not a fighter! Ya want ta see a fighter?
SHELLY: I just want us ta go home now. That's all I want...
DWAYNE: *(lets go)* Yeah! So ya can say I'm not agressive! Ya say I'm not a fighter?
SHELLY: Oh, you're so tough, are ya?
DWAYNE: At least I had the guts ta come here an fuckin make bets! Did you ever?
SHELLY: Oh, it takes guts, does it? Ta lose everythin we got on a horse race?
DWAYNE: Well, you're gonna get it back. If it's the last thing I ever do!

[*DWAYNE starts to exit.*]

SHELLY: How'd ya get so sick, baby?

DWAYNE: I ain't sick! Don't say I'm sick! I never took a sick day in my life!

SHELLY: I know ya didn't. I know you're good.

DWAYNE: Yeah. You'd like it if I was sick. You'd have more power over me then, eh?

SHELLY: I don't wanna have any power over ya. I just want to go home.

[*HE stops.*]

DWAYNE: Shel? I can't ever go home again...

SHELLY: Dwayne. You're scarin me. Please...

DWAYNE: I think I did...a terrible thing tonight. I didn't know... what I was doin...

SHELLY: I know. But, we can deal with it, can't we? We can try...

DWAYNE: Ya don't even know. When you find out, you'll never love me again.

SHELLY: What?

[*pause*]

DWAYNE: Ya don't even know what the terrible thing is, yet.

[*HE disappears into the darkness.*]

SCENE 7

Outside the stables. The sound of horses, rustling in their stalls. A solitary light over the stable's locked *door*. DWAYNE sits on a crate. SHELLY comes near.

SHELLY: Dwayne?

DWAYNE: I told ya. Get lost! What are ya comin spookin around for? Get home!

SHELLY: I finally found ya in the pitch fuckin dark an I'm not goin home without ya!

[*pause*]

DWAYNE: If ya want ta hang out at the stables then.

SHELLY: Dwayne. It's gettin really late. Will ya please give this up an come home?

DWAYNE: I ain't givin nothin up. It's started, an it's gonna be finished.

SHELLY: What's the terrible thing ya did? What else did ya lose?

[*pause*]

DWAYNE: You'll find out.

SHELLY: Baby. I know ya got a sickness. Ya just want ta hurt somethin.

DWAYNE: I don't got any sickness! Don't say that!

SHELLY: No. It's like my sickness. Somethin like. You're sick an ya don't know it.

DWAYNE: That's a loada shit. Ya think you're so high falutin. Ya know everythin.

SHELLY: Why don't ya come home. An let me take carea ya?

[*pause*]

DWAYNE: I ain't crippled like you. I don't need any nurse-
maid.

SHELLY: Okay. Dwayne. Sure! You don't got a sickness
then...

DWAYNE: I don't. I'm as normal as anyone.

SHELLY: You're perfectly fuckin normal. Ya just lost our whole
savings...

DWAYNE: I took a risk. Ya can't get anywhere in life if ya
don't risk. That ain't sick.

SHELLY: Na. You ain't sick at all. You're sittin here outside the stable at midnight...

DWAYNE: I'm gonna get your money back. I told ya you're
gonna get it!

SHELLY: ...Cause you're waitin ta kill the guy who combs
the fuckin horses!

DWAYNE: I'm gonna hit you if you keep sayin I got a sickness! You're pushin me!

SHELLY: You touch me again, you're gonna have two fuckin
broken arms!

[*The horses in the stalls erupt.*]

DWAYNE: Yeah? Ya think ya can break my arms, do ya?

SHELLY: Yeah. Y'll look pretty funny tryin ta wipe your
ass with your foot!

[*pause*]

DWAYNE: Please go home. Okay? I don't want ya ta be
here for this.

SHELLY: I ain't goin home without my husband.

DWAYNE: Ya don't want me for your husband. Ya deserve
a lot better.

[*pause*]

SHELLY: Ya were just tryin to solve all our troubles.

DWAYNE: I win sometimes. I never had a big win. But I win. I wanted ya ta see me.

SHELLY: I know. Ya took all that money cause...

DWAYNE: I wouldn'ta ever took it. Except, I know. I'm enough of a burden already.

SHELLY: I know it's killin ya. That ya gotta be supported right now. But it's okay...

DWAYNE: We woulda had over thirty five hundred dollars, Shel. It was so close.

SHELLY: Remember what we said before. This ain't forever.

DWAYNE: If if it wasn't for that stupid fuckin shitty tip. That stupid bastard...

SHELLY: Dwayne. I'm really scared you're gonna get hurt if ya stay here.

DWAYNE: Quit sayin I'm gonna get hurt! You're sayin I can't take carea myself!

SHELLY: I ain't sayin that. Dwayne, I know the state you're in, you'll probly kill him.

DWAYNE: You're fuckin right I will. I can handle myself just fine.

SHELLY: But you been losin weight. Ya must weigh half what ya did six months ago.

DWAYNE: That's got nothin ta do with anythin. I won't take any shit from him.

[*pause*]

SHELLY: Aren't ya hungry right now? I know ya must be hungry. I always am.

DWAYNE: Just go home if ya want ta eat. I ain't goin. It's that simple.

SHELLY: We got lotsa food at home. There's some burgers in the freezer. An soup.

DWAYNE: I ain't hungry. I don't need any food.

SHELLY: I'll tell ya what. I'll even cook for ya. You could run us a little bubble bath.

DWAYNE: I can't go back there. Ya don't want me to go back there!

SHELLY: Dwayne. We won't get evicted...We can talk ta the landlord. No one'll know.

DWAYNE: I ain't goin back unless I can get ya your money. That's final.

SHELLY: If we haveta go ta welfare, it's only for a month. We can deal with it.

DWAYNE: Maybe you can deal with it. I ain't dealin with it. I can't...

SHELLY: No one'll ever know. Your Da'll never haveta find out.

DWAYNE: He'll know. He knows I can't pull my weight. I can't support my family.

SHELLY: Karen. We're gonna haveta pay Karen from the sofa. We can do that.

DWAYNE: The sofa. How we gonna pay her from the sofa?

SHELLY: Yeah. There's always a buncha quarters an loonies in between the cushions.

DWAYNE: There is?

SHELLY: Yeah. When we lay there cuddlin up. We always lose some down there.

DWAYNE: I love you so much, Shel. This was all for you...

SHELLY: If there's no money there, she'll understand. We'll just tell her a few days.

DWAYNE: We'll have a worse fuckin reputation than her if we stiff her.

SHELLY: We'll talk to her. She's got a heart. We won't tell her what happened here.

DWAYNE: We won't haveta tell anyone anythin. Cause I'm gettin it all back.

[*pause*]

SHELLY: This is just another gamble for ya, isn't it? Ya got no money ta make a bet...

DWAYNE: Leave me alone. I don't deserve your trouble!

SHELLY: ...So you're gonna put your life on the line. Please. Give this up...

DWAYNE: My life ain't worth nothin anyway. I may's well go out fightin.

SHELLY: Don't ya understand, though? If you're on the line, we're there too.

DWAYNE: I ain't givin nothin up. I don't give up. Everyone knows that about me!

[*pause*]

SHELLY: I know ya gave somethin up once. Didn't ya? I remember...

DWAYNE: What did I ever give up? Tell me what I ever gave up.

SHELLY: Ya gave up smokin. Didn't ya? We both did.

DWAYNE: That's different. That ain't the same thing as this.

SHELLY: Ya remember why ya gave up smokin? Dwayne?

[*SHE moves closer to him.*]

DWAYNE: So. What're ya sayin? So what I gave up smokin?

SHELLY: It was for the baby, wasn't it? Wasn't it?

DWAYNE: Yeah. I gave that up for the baby. Ya know that.

SHELLY: I know. An it was hard for ya. I know it was. To give it up.

DWAYNE: It wasn't that hard. I been through worse.

SHELLY: Ya were strong too. Ya gave it up cold turkey. Soon as I got pregnant.

DWAYNE: I thought ya looked beautiful pregnant.

SHELLY: We didn't want our little darlin ta come outta me with two heads, did we?

DWAYNE: No. It was dangerous to her health.

SHELLY: We could barely decide on one name for her. If we'da had two to deal with...

102

DWAYNE: We don't need to talk about her now, do we? She's home safe.

SHELLY: Yeah. An she needs her daddy home, too. That's what she needs.

[*pause*]

DWAYNE: I...can't.

SHELLY: We can get better. We can always get better. We just can't do it here.

DWAYNE: *(vicious)* I ain't sick. I ain't sick! Why do ya keep tryin ta tell me I'm sick?

[*HE stumbles away, onto the track.*]

SHELLY: If you make me go home alone tonight, we're finished! *(pause)* GO TA HELL!

[*The horses in the stalls are going insane, as DWAYNE disappears.*]

SCENE 8

On the track. SHELLY leans against the rail, waiting. DWAYNE walks into view, head down.

SHELLY: That's six times I chased ya around the track Dwayne. I counted.

DWAYNE: Stop followin me if ya can't take it. I thought ya were gonna leave!

SHELLY: *(ignoring)* I ain't as strong as you. I'm only in shape for waitressin.

DWAYNE: Get home! Why don't ya just get home an get away from me!

SHELLY: Ya really want me ta walk home alone? Through
town. At this hour.

DWAYNE: I don't care. I don't care what ya do.

SHELLY: I know that isn't you talkin. The guy I married,
he'd never...

DWAYNE: Go find someone else. I don't care...

SHELLY: He doesn't even like me checkin the mailbox alone.
He protects me.

DWAYNE: You can find someone else ta protect ya. That's
if ya already haven't!

[*pause*]

SHELLY: What's that supposedta mean?

DWAYNE: Onea your army boys. They'll take carea ya better than I could.

SHELLY: I don't want onea them. I love you. I only love
you.

DWAYNE: They got the big pockets ya love so much. They
wouldn't mind protectin ya.

SHELLY: Ya don't have ta talk dirty ta me. Ya think I'm some
kinda pig?

DWAYNE: I just..want ya ta be happy. I bet that'd make ya
happy, wouldn't it?

SHELLY: I ain't lettin ya pass me. We're goin home now if
I haveta drag ya there.

DWAYNE: I'm goin back to the stables. They should be
comin back around now.

SHELLY: You're not goin back there. I'm not lettin you kill
yourself!

[*pause*]

DWAYNE: I'll show ya. I'll fuckin walk the whole way
around then...

SHELLY: Will ya think about your daughter? Will ya think
about that, please?

DWAYNE: Why can't ya see that I'm doin this for us?

SHELLY: Melissa isn't gonna be better off without a father! What matters to you?

DWAYNE: Maybe she will be better off. Without a father like me.

[*HE starts to walk away.*]

SHELLY: Ya always say I'm the one who runs away from things? Who's runnin now?

DWAYNE: I ain't runnin away. I never ran away from anythin in my life!

SHELLY: Look at ya. All you're doin is runnin around in circles.

DWAYNE: I don't run away from trouble. I told ya where I'm goin, an I'm goin there.

SHELLY: This ain't for us, it's for you. This is just another risk you're takin an it's us.

DWAYNE: Well, I ain't runnin away, that's for sure.

SHELLY: I know. Dwayne never runs away. He's so strong...

DWAYNE: I don't. You know I don't.

SHELLY: It's your sickness makin ya run away from everythin!

DWAYNE: There's no fuckin sickness! I ain't sick! I'm normal.

SHELLY: Ya think you're bein so cool. Ya think you're bein such a strong man.

DWAYNE: Go to hell with ya...

[*HE keeps going, not looking back.*]

SHELLY: Your baby is home! What about your baby? Can ya think about her? *Please...*

DWAYNE: You don't know how much I'm thinkin about her right now.

SHELLY: You ain't strong! You ain't strong at all! You're a coward!

[*HE stops dead.*]

DWAYNE: What did ya call me? Did you call me a coward?

SHELLY: Ya keep sayin, ya keep sayin, ya got...everythin's under control!

DWAYNE: I do. I got everythin under control here. You're the one outta control.

SHELLY: Yeah. Ya think ya got control of anythin? That's such a joke. Can't ya see?

DWAYNE: What can't I see? What do ya think ya can show me that I can't see?

SHELLY: You don't got any control of anythin. Not even yourself. Can't ya see that?

DWAYNE: I got controlla this situation! Why can't *you* see that?

SHELLY: You don't even got control of...

[*silence*]

DWAYNE: What? I don't got control of what? Say it!

SHELLY: Ya don't. Do ya? An ya don't even know it. Ya can't see...what's happenin...

DWAYNE: What are you sayin? Are you talkin about us in bed?

SHELLY: Cause you'd rather...gamble than make love to your wife, wouldn't ya?

[*HE approaches her.*]

DWAYNE: Is that what ya think? Is that why ya been followin me?

SHELLY: It's cause you're always here aren't ya? Even when you're home with us...

DWAYNE: So. You're in heat. So that's what this is all about.

SHELLY: Huh?

DWAYNE: Ya think I'd rather gamble than fuck. Ya think I can't fuck anymore?

[*HE unbuckles his trousers.*]

SHELLY: What do ya think you're doin? I didn't mean...ta
    be cruel...
DWAYNE: I'm gonna prove somethin to ya, Shel. I can fuck
    ya whenever I want!
SHELLY: No ya can't. Ya can't do that. Ya aren't gonna do
    that...
DWAYNE: Ya want a good fuck? I'll give ya a fuck. I'll
    give ya a good ride.
SHELLY: Dwayne...if ya try anythin, I'll scream...
DWAYNE: No one's gonna hear ya from way out here. But
    I'll make ya scream.
SHELLY: Get away from me...I hate you!
DWAYNE: I'll make ya love me! I'll make ya love me so
    much!
SHELLY: No ya won't! I hate you...
DWAYNE: I hate you, too!
SHELLY: I hate you forever...!

[*HE throws her onto the track.*]

DWAYNE: You're in heat. We're both in heat. Why ya
    fightin? Let's fuck!
SHELLY: (*paralyzed*) Dwayne..?

[*HE sits astride her, ripping at her pants. HE tries to enter
her, but can't. HE gets very upset, confused. HE becomes
aware that SHE has stopped struggling.*]

[*Faraway, the horses are heard in their stalls. THEY stare at
each other for a long time, trying to remember.*]

SHELLY: (*soft*) Ya threw me...in...shit. There's...sh-
    shit...underneath.

[*pause*]

DWAYNE: Baby..?

SHELLY: I love ya so much...I...

DWAYNE: I didn't...mean...I...

SHELLY: But...I haveta...get up...now. I can't stay with ya
here.

[*pause*]

DWAYNE: I'm...s-sorry...I'm...so sorry...

SHELLY: Dwayne...

DWAYNE: I don't know...what I'm doin.

SHELLY: We haveta get up now. We can't stay here.
We'll...die here.

[*SHE gets up, slowly.*]

DWAYNE: How could ya ever love me now?

[*pause*]

SHELLY: I...don't know.

DWAYNE: How?

[*pause*]

SHELLY: I guess...I got no control either.

[*SHE helps him, as HE tries to stand up.*]

SCENE 9

The bench. SHELLY and DWAYNE sitting. DWAYNE is very still, strange. SHELLY is cleaning him off as best she can.

SHELLY: We're gonna haveta go to a gas station. To get some soap.
DWAYNE: Yeah.
SHELLY: No one's gonna pick us up hikin covered in this stuff, are they?
DWAYNE: No one's gonna pick us up.
SHELLY: People that pick up hitchhikers might have a problem with that. Huh?
DWAYNE: We need to clean off. We need to fix ourselves up.
SHELLY: That's for the miracle of detergent. Shit comes out. Like everythin else.

[*SHE rises. HE stays seated.*]

DWAYNE: Yeah...
SHELLY: C'mon. Get up. We're gonna go now.
DWAYNE: We're gonna walk?
SHELLY: Yeah. It ain't...that far really. As the crow flies.
DWAYNE: Do ya...love me, Shel?
SHELLY: I love you. You know I do.
DWAYNE: How much?
SHELLY: More than anythin.
DWAYNE: Really?

[*pause*]

SHELLY: What's wrong now?
DWAYNE: We need...a miracle.
SHELLY: Why?
DWAYNE: Because of...the thing...that I did...

[*DWAYNE starts to cry. The sound of hooves, distant.*]

SHELLY: What is it? Whatever it is, tell me now.
DWAYNE: Ya don't know...how sick I am! Ya don't...
SHELLY: Dwayne. Tell me.
DWAYNE: I need help. I need someone to help me. I don't
    know why...
SHELLY: I'll help ya. If this thing is so terrible a thing, ya
    better tell me!
DWAYNE: Swear you'll always love me forever.
SHELLY: I do. It's probably not that bad, baby. Just tell me
    what it is. How much more money?

[*pause*]

DWAYNE: I was...gonna find a way...ta get home first. Cause
    we were supposedta win...
SHELLY: Yeah...? Keep goin...

[*HE cracks. It is a torrent.*]

DWAYNE: We haveta go home. And there's no...there's...no...
SHELLY: No...what?
DWAYNE: No...no...sitter...no...
SHELLY: What?
DWAYNE: There's no one there. There's...no one.
    Just...empty. Just...

[*silence*]

SHELLY: How..?

DWAYNE: How could ya ever love me now? How much...do
ya love me now? How much..?

[*The sound of hooves, thunderous. Bearing down. Relentless.*]

[*THEY do not give way.*]

Blackout

END

AFTERWORD

BY DR. ROD NICHOLLS

In Heartspent and Black Silence Shelly says to her husband Dwayne 'we're going to get outta the hole sweetie,' but the world they share with the three characters in Joyride is a bleak, post-industrial hole from which there is no escape. Not one of them is over twenty-five and their situation is summed up in the simple logic spitted out by Joyride's Craig: 'We are shit. We're broke. That mean's we're shit.' Craig is on probation and unemployed, while Rachel earns minimum wage clerking at the convenience store as does Jess working for his father's seasonal landscaping business. In Heartspent and Black Silence Dwayne is on his last week of unemployment and Shelly is a waitress. In Cape Breton's understanding of itself, the suffering of oppression, unemployment or material hardship is always recognized, but this pain can be tempered by other influences. The family might not be able to eliminate indignities of the present inflicted by others, but it can provide a refuge. Especially when families tap into the deep cultural tradition in which they are rooted, this refuge can become a kind of spiritual reality which redeems the rest of life. With stripped-down, pitch perfect dialogue, Michael Melski, by contrast, captures the grinding feel of dead-ended lives which are cut off from any past.

Melski's plays are certainly not the first to explore the darker side of Cape Breton life. Daniel MacIvor's Present Time and Audrey Butler's Black Friday, to give two examples, are moving and uninhibited explorations of the depth and consequences of repressed family conflicts and violence. In each case, the darkness is inseparable from the family dynamics which control the flow of the action, undermining any distinction between life and death, personal and political. The lure of reconciliation and the possibility of a new life for the survivors is part of the attraction of these plays. The characters in <u>Joyride</u> and <u>Heartspent and Black Silence</u> do have families and some have fed the self-destructive motives of their children (in the case of Rachel, Craig and Dwayne). Still, they no more have a role in the dramatic action than those apparently decent families who are impotent to change their children's future for the better (in the case of Jess and Shelly). It is a jarring experience to enter a Cape Breton world with such an atmosphere of complete homelessness.

<u>Joyride's</u> characters, for instance, move from one Sydney location to the next, always gravitating to a smoky Tim Horton's because the poker machines and pool tables elsewhere require constant supplies of money. Tim Horton's is the inevitable destination of a threesome who believe: 'We could go anywhere. But there's nowhere.' Where does this leave home? A vague somewhere beyond the periphery of the action to which characters drift away and then reappear. Quite appropriately, it is Jess' Roger Whittaker loving mother, not Craig's abusive father nor Rachel's promiscuous mother who has the greatest presence in the play. But she only appears in the form of her K-car (needed for the 'getaway') or as the little statue of the Virgin Mary on its dashboard which can be put out of sight when necessary. In Dan's Dairy, however, the tendency for physical things or places to absorb and yet reflect the loss of connections develops to bizarre proportions. The Dairy starts out as the convenient target of Craig's simple robbery plan: Rachel works there, thinks there is $40,000 in the safe, and can leave the door open when her shift ends; but by the end of the play when he finds out that Rachel had made a mistake, Craig stands by the $400.00 and says 'my whole life is here.' He is referring to himself, but 'Dan's Dairy' has enveloped and crushed all three.

Rachel and Jess originally object to Craig's plan by emphasizing that 'it's our store.' This just makes explicit that the more Rachel and Jess' future prospects have diminished, the more Dan's Dairy has come to act as a medium of shared identity. Along with Craig, they grew up in and around the store, and two of them never left. Rachel now works for Dan, putting up with his cheap ways and ignorant harassment. Dan lets Jess, the youngest one as it were, hang around when Rachel is working because he can be taken for a little money when he has any and always submits to his authority. The Dairy, therefore, takes on an incestuous look which is magnified when Craig returns and Rachel tells him what she has seen. Craig is obsessed with the memory of being cheated out of his 'achievement' of winning on the Dairy's poker machines. It was his father who had put him 'on a dog's leash' after he received a distorted version of the incident from Dan, but the memory of his father immediately disappears into a larger than life image of Dan: an authority figure as dirty old man, exploiting anyone who doesn't realize that 'everything's fucking rigged' to satisfy the old man's needs. So the way Rachel and Jess express their objections to Craig's plan merely feeds his obsessional vision of the corrupt patriarch who deserves to be robbed and in which the exploited children are his rightful beneficiaries. Unfortunately they can't perceive the logic of this delusion which eventually leads to the conclusion that death is just retribution for Dan.

In <u>Heartspent and Black Silence</u> Dwayne and Shelly are married with a young baby, Melissa, but this just seems to sharpen the edge on the form of homelessness from which they suffer. Shelly can't see their dingy, claustrophobic, basement apartment as anything other than a lurking killer because she suspects it is being poisoned by a gas leak. Dwayne thinks she is just paranoid although unemployment has made the apartment his prison. Both crave an escape from this place which is not really their own. Shelly would settle for a night out at the Triple Cinemas, but Dwayne's more elaborate escape plan takes them to seedy, smelly Tartan Downs racetrack which is the single setting for the play. The world appears in Tartan Downs no differently than at Dan's Dairy: Dwayne has come to assume, like Craig, that everything is rigged and

'No one can beat a rigged game. No matter how good you are.' Dwayne, however, has his own strategy for coping in a world where skill and effort are irrelevant. He has thrown in his lot with those people who are in on the fix, putting every last cent on Black Silence on the basis of insider information about horse doping. This is a nothing left to lose in more than one sense, because Dwayne has already decided that nothing can justify moving back in with Shelly's parents since their dignity as a family now rests on the fact of their bare independence. The moment it becomes apparent that he has abandoned the baby, therefore, the squalor of Tartan Downs closes in and defines them: two isolated individuals desperately clinging to each other, though not even their words connect.

What pleasure can a person take in watching these sad characters move toward self-destruction? Aside from anything else, both plays are funny. It's been noted, for instance, that the 'dark truths' they convey means 'this is a picture of Cape Breton ... that doesn't enter into the Cape Breton Summertime Revue' (The Chronicle Herald, 1/9/94, C6). Things are more complicated than that. Heard out of context, in fact, much of the banter in Melski's plays is intriguingly Revue-like. As Heartspent and Black Silence is starting, Dwayne claims to 'know a bit about horse racin' but Shelly points out that 'I had ta explain the Pick-three lotto to ya five times,' and when she says 'I ain't gonna be your date if ya plan on losin your shirt' Dwayne comes back with 'Ya have ta be my date. We're married.' Before we sense Melissa's fate, the couple's rambling but fragmentary expressions of parental paranoia or affection are especially funny. Shelly, for instance, admires Dwayne for giving up smoking cold turkey when she got pregnant: 'We didn't want our little darlin ta come outta me with two heads, did we? ... Cause, we could barely decide on one name for her. If we'da had two ... .'

In Joyride the lines are cruder and more smart-ass funny, but imagine listening to some of them delivered by characters in the radically different context of a skit aiming at pure laughter and having no relationship to an overarching plot. Then once more a family resemblance to 'the picture of Cape Breton' in the Revue emerges, and the comic identity is worth noting even though lines, character and context are obviously inseparable. In fact, Melski's success at balancing our ignorance and knowledge of the developing story is largely due to the dialogue's comic texture, because this is what stamps Shelly, Dwayne and the others as immediately recognizable Cape Breton characters. As a result, we bracket unease at dangerous signs or even repress the significance of explicit statements, and fix on the disarming ordinariness of the characters. More accurately, through the first half of both plays their blend of sharp but dopey humor lightens and leavens their otherwise depressing plight. This draws us into their perspective where we remain even after the 'plans' have been revealed as full-blown delusions and the very possibility of comic moments has been obliterated.

Watching the painful endings might not even be devoid of pleasure. If the believability of Melski's characters consists in our ability to recognize ordinary people in them, then the sight of such characters twisted and crushed by powerful self-deception and simple mistakes through the course of a play, can be frightening. Still, according to Aristotle, Greek tragedy worked by representing action which evoked the audience's pity and fear, and when the dramatic resolution purged that pity and fear a special sort of pleasure was produced: the pleasure of catharsis. Arthur Miller argued that plays about 'the common man' could just as easily provoke this cathartic effect as plays about royalty or noble dignitaries, so this line of interpretation makes some sense. However, in an otherwise enthusiastic review of the Atlantic Fringe Festival's production of Joyride, Christopher Majka suggests that the play lacks a cathartic conclusion: 'I like virtually everything about this play - except for its conclusion. This play masterfully builds its dramatic tension until - at the final moment when a climactic catharsis should take place - it simpers to a kind of non-conclusion' (Theatrum, Feb\Mar 95, #42, p.30). This is strong criticism and it is best addressed by examining how Melski builds the dramatic tension in the first place.

By the end of <u>Joyride</u>, the audience, like Rachel and Jess, is gripped by uncertainty regarding Craig's real intentions, but the tension was originally generated by Rachel and Jess' hesitating but inevitable decision to enter the plan. The play starts (as well as ends) with the two on stage by themselves, and the only way that Craig's plan gets moving is by tying into and exploiting the relationship between Rachel and Jess. This is really a simple story of unrequited love. A successful production of the play, for instance, would have to establish a distinctive emotional tone for their interaction in the first scene, and then elaborate it in later ones: unless we see the awkwardness of the departure from Tim Horton's at the end of scene three, there is no possibility of comprehending the necessity of Jess' acquiescence to Craig's plan in the following two scenes. Jess does not go along because of something as abstract as peer pressure, rather Rachel kisses him and says she really needs him. In her relationship with Craig as well as Jess, Rachel's motivations are more complex. When Craig moves the timing ahead Rachel goes along, but it's certainly not as if she is turning away from Jess (once more) to Craig, because the words with which she seals her fate — 'I can handle anything you got!' — contain a good deal of spite.

In <u>Heartspent and Black Silence</u>, by contrast, tension is derived from the slow torture of Shelly coming to recognize the facts of Dwayne's dangerous plan. She is in an impossible situation. What most of us call ordinary reality is supported and nourished by a past, and enlivened by dreams and plans which open up that past into a future. Take away the future and ordinary reality does not just become intolerable; there is a human tendency for it to be more or less squeezed out of existence. Without a good amount of courage and luck, in other words, what is intolerable can spawn wishes and dreams which mutate into all sorts of delusions. Shelly's alternate response is sickness. The suffering life causes her has many symptoms. Dwayne can't understand them anymore than Shelly, precisely because sickness (like Dwayne's gambling) is her distinctively irrational way of coping. It's not coincidental that when <u>Joyride's</u> Jess is first confronted with Craig's plan he blocks it out with a fury that can only be expressed with 'I'm sick! I'm fucking sick!' repeated over and over again. He is motivated solely by the perfectly natural complexity of his feelings for Rachel, but in the absence of effective, countervailing motivations these feelings spiral him into either Craig's reality or a retreat into sickness.

This absence or emptiness, which is at the center of the existence of all these characters, does not mean Rachel, Jess, Craig, Shelly and Dwayne do not feel (because they feel strongly); rather they are impaled on their emotions — locked out of any family, community or cultural past which could give life a horizon for healthy growth. This is expressed most directly in the elemental realism of the dialogue in which <u>Joyride</u> and <u>Heartspent and Black Silence</u> is written: throughout both plays there is only a single occasion when speech is not contained within one line; and the words are tied so ruthlessly to the fragmented surface of the characters' consciousness that someone might question the status of these plays as literature as opposed to dramatic scripts. The form, however, is corrosively authentic. And it is fitting, therefore, that as the action comes to an end, the audience hears the hard, fragile surface of speech breaking down completely. Rachel, in shock, doesn't know where she is and cannot complete a sentence; Jess tries to support her with short variations of 'don't worry, I'm here.' In <u>Heartspent and Black Silence</u> Shelly, too, can only express her incomprehension in stuttering and incomplete questions.

The disintegration of speech is complemented and focused in stage images of degradation: Shelly and Dwayne sit penni-

119

less at the closed track covered in horseshit; Rachel and Jess stagger to the K-car while Craig, still in the Dairy spattered with Dan's blood, madly plays a game on a rigged machine 'for old time's sake.' Jess finally seems confident playing the role of Rachel's protector and comforter, but his decision to participate in the robbery makes this as delusionary as anything in Craig's head. Majka suggests that Joyride lacked a 'climactic catharsis,' but surely all this brings both plays to a fittingly chilling and cathartic close. What were the dramatic options? Place Craig, with his knife, in a stand-off with Sydney police? Give him a monologue as a vehicle to elaborate his fascination with the justification of his crime like some Dostoevski character? It's simply that the soaring, poetic monologues which give Bryden MacDonald's plays their literary lustre would be out of place in the mouths of any character in these plays. Using such a device to draw the audience into the final depths of depravity would go against the real revelation: there is no depth, only a vacuum. To have Craig turn more and more away from Jess, and start to address his same short aggressive pieces of speech to the pocker machine is to represent his state far more effectively.

It's understandable that some people will have a moral resistance to the cathartic effect of <u>Joyride</u> and <u>Heartspent and Black Silence</u>. Part of it is that with characters like Craig and Dwayne at center-stage there is the belief that the suffering of the victims has been compromised. It is noteworthy, perhaps, that Dan and Melissa never appear on stage. Pointing out that Shelly is also a victim doesn't help here because she is innocent but ever so passive. When Arthur Miller thought of appropriate heroes for this 'age of the common man' he expressed one defining characteristic: 'an inherent unwillingness to remain passive in the face of what he conceives to be a challenge to his dignity, his image of his rightful status.' And it's not hard to look past a Willy Loman or Tom Joad and come up with Cape Breton characters who embody that characteristic strength — the women in <u>Margaret's Museum</u>.

120

When we hear Craig ('We're fucking born ripped off. There's right and wrong.') and Dwayne ('Ya can't get anywhere in life if ya don't risk.'), don't we hear only punk-loser parodies of a striving for dignity?

Robbery and gambling problems are no doubt promoted by Cape Breton's economic conditions, but there is something deeply unsatisfying in the sociological explanations of self-proclaimed experts in the aftermath of a robbery, or evening of gambling gone wrong. If the level of generality keeps causal explanations on the outside, a dramatic attempt to represent things from the perspective of the participants, means taking seriously the outlook of a punk and loser (as well as those who are guilty by association). For this loaded language merely sums up what they do: one murders an acquaintance for $400, and the other abandons his child for a night of gambling. In the case of Craig and Dwayne, then, an overwhelming sense of their own impotence in a world rigged against them, has created the belief that reality can be transformed only by 'plans' founded on simple luck and all or nothing risk. What they see as good luck within this belief, may be nothing more than a mundane perceptual error or naive trust, although once accepted, self-deception takes over and transforms every incident — the timing of Craig's return, Shelly's lucky bet on Heartspent — into a 'sign' that what they know will happen, was 'fated' to happen. This is the replacement for a world in which effort, striving and work have significance, and family, community and imagination provide consolation for failed or thwarted effort.

From within the world represented in these two plays, to take the risk is the only way to claim one's dignity. They make this clear without contradicting the moral point of view: we are repelled not only by the consequences of these attempts to claim 'dignity,' but also by the recognition that any strength of character is reduced to Craig and Dwayne's rock-bottom faith in 'plans' which have little connection with reality. (Weakness is not an excuse, even for Dwayne's 'addiction,' as Shelly calls it). So why the moral resistance? I think the sheer authenticity of the plays forces us to consider whether these particular characters could have claimed their dignity in any way we would consider legitimate. She might not have become a criminal, but if Craig had stayed in Dartmouth, where would Rachel's 'dream' of a camaro have taken her in life? If Dwayne had taken Shelly to the Sheraton Casino to be duped with more style than at Tartan Downs would it have made any difference?

Practically, of course, we have to go on making moral (and legal) judgments which assume that all people have options consistent with real dignity. Still, stick with these characters. Underlying all the ignorance, self-deception and punk-loser attitude, what if Craig and Dwayne's basic assumption that the world is rigged is true? At the very least we might occasionally do a double-take and glimpse a life which is empty and dangerously futile — but not nothing.